STRIKEFORCE AGENT
VALERIE INGLEWOOD

BAD INTENT

T.K. WILDE

Dreamstone Publishing © 2017

www.dreamstonepublishing.com

ISBN: 1925499294

ISBN-13:   978-1-925499-29-2

Disclaimer

This is a work of fiction. Any resemblance to persons living or deceased is purely coincidental, and is not intended.

BAD INTENT

Dedication

To my readers – without you, there would be no stories.

To all of my family and friends, who support me when I am writing, and make it possible for books to get finished – thank you!

Table of Contents

Chapter 1

Colonel Tomlinson stood behind his desk. He wore plain green army fatigues and lace-up black boots, and he struck quite a contrast to Valerie and Charlene with their pressed business suits and manicured nails. But he stood ramrod erect, and his muscled shoulders strained against his cotton shirt. He could beat any member of the Strikeforce Team on the obstacle course, the shooting range, in the sparring ring, or on a written test.

He held up a case file.

"This is gonna be a tough one, even for you two. I would assign Jeff and Tiko to work with you again, since you did so well together last time. But they're not back from Florida yet, so we're bringing in another expert to help you out."

"Who is it?" Valerie asked.

"He's a law enforcement officer from another high-level investigation unit," Colonel Tomlinson replied. "They're stationed in Arizona, so they work mostly on cross-border cases. But they're even more prestigious and elite than we are. As a matter of fact, they're so hush-hush, you've probably never heard of them."

Valerie and Charlene exchanged glances.

"I'm sure I've heard of them," Charlene remarked. "I've been in this business long enough to know just about everybody from the top down."

"Not even you know about these guys," the Colonel told her. "These guys don't work with anybody. They keep their activities strictly confidential."

"Then why are they working with us now?" Valerie asked.

"One of their suspects escaped," Colonel Tomlinson replied.

"They caught him in Laredo and were transporting him back across the border to San Antonio when he escaped again. He made it as far north as Flagstaff, but he was murdered in his room at the Lamplighter Motel before our friends could catch him. Now this expert is investigating his death, and you two are going to help him. Or, I should say, he's going to be helping you. We've been officially assigned the case, but because of the nature of the incident, we're working together on this."

Valerie's eyebrows went up.

"It's a little out of order, isn't it? We've never worked with any other agency before, and if these guys are that elite and that confidential, they won't take kindly to sharing their territory with us. If they already had this guy in custody and let him get away, they'll be on edge about it happening again."

"They won't be on edge about it happening again, because he's dead," Colonel Tomlinson replied.

"But they might be on edge about you making a mess of their investigation. I admit it's a recipe for disaster, and I wouldn't agree to it under normal circumstances. The only reason I am agreeing to it is because they've specially requested this. It seems word of your exploits has traveled through the agencies of this great land. They want your help."

Charlene jerked her head at Valerie.

"It's Valerie's exploits that have traveled, not mine. I've been on the Strikeforce Team long enough, and they never specially requested me. They must want to see Valerie in action."

Colonel Tomlinson grinned.

"Something like that."

Valerie eyed the file in his hand.

"I guess one murder is very like another. We'll work our mojo and solve it, and everyone will be suitably impressed. I only have one question."

"Shoot," the Colonel replied.

"What's the name of this elite investigation unit?" she asked.

"The feds call 'em XQT06," Colonel Tomlinson replied. "But they call themselves the O-Line."

"The O-Line?" Valerie repeated. "That's football slang for the Offensive Line. Why do they call themselves that?"

"They consider themselves the first line of attack in the war across the border," Colonel Tomlinson replied.

"They view the tide of illegals coming across the border as an invasion force, and they see themselves as the front line battalion tasked with repelling that attack."

"Wouldn't that make them the Defensive Line?" Valerie asked.

Colonel Tomlinson shrugged.

"I didn't make up the name. Maybe you can ask your expert yourself. He's coming in to meet you and brief you on the case."

"When?" Charlene asked.

A bell sounded on a tablet computer sitting on Colonel Tomlinson's desk. He bent over it and touched the screen.

"He's here now."

At that moment, the door opened, and a clean-cut man in an immaculate suit strolled into the office. Valerie froze.

"This is Captain Dan Henderson," Colonel Tomlinson told them. "I believe you know each other."

Dan walked right up to Valerie, took her by the hand, and kissed her on the cheek. "We know each other."

Valerie turned bright red, but she couldn't stop smiling at him. For some reason, she didn't take her hand out of his grasp. He gazed down into her eyes with a big grin on his face.

"It's good to see you again, Valerie. I didn't think I would see you again so soon."

Valerie's cheeks burned.

"So, you're the one who specially requested that we work on this case."

"I didn't request you because I wanted to see you again," Dan replied. "I wanted to see you again, but I wouldn't use this case to give myself an excuse to track you down. I could have done that anytime. We've had a devil of a time with this case. I was impressed with the way you cracked that EdenCloud case, so I thought we couldn't do any better than to get your help on this."

Valerie dropped her eyes.

"I didn't do anything special at EdenCloud, or on any other case. I've always had help from... from everybody."

Charlene stepped forward and extended her hand.

"It's good to see you again, Dan. I trust you're putting your father's death behind you. You must be if you're working on cases like this."

Dan shook hands with Charlene, but he didn't kiss her on the cheek.

"Yes, I'm back at work, now that my father is resting peacefully in our family burial plot in Phoenix. My family owes you and Valerie a huge debt of gratitude for the work you did to bring his killer to justice."

Valerie dropped her voice to a murmur.

"Maybe you haven't heard. AngelPie is in a care home for mentally ill teenagers in Missouri. I wouldn't exactly call what happened to her bringing a killer to justice. She's as much a victim of EdenCloud as your father was."

"That's exactly what I mean," Dan returned. "I heard what happened to her. I've followed every single one of those people since the retreat center broke up. What happened to AngelPie was the closest thing to justice we could ever hope for. She's getting the treatment she needs, and all the other crooked members of that loopy outfit are getting what they deserve, too. I heard her mother got audited by the IRS and lost every dime she had."

Valerie suppressed a snicker.

"I heard that, too."

Colonel Tomlinson cleared his throat.

"Well, if you people are finished catching up on old times, perhaps you could take a walk into the briefing room and get started on the present. The body ain't gettin' any colder, if you know what I mean."

Dan bit back a smile.

"Yes, Sir. If you don't mind, Sir, we'll take the case file with us."

Colonel Tomlinson handed him the file.

"By all means. I was just about to give it to Charlene when you showed up. If you need anything else, don't hesitate to let me know."

"Thank you, Sir." Dan did everything short of saluting before he, Valerie and Charlene left the office.

Outside, Charlene gestured toward a room two doors down the hall.

"This is the briefing room. You can give us the details in here."

The three investigators took their places around the table in the middle of the room. Dan opened the case file and laid a big black and white mug shot in front of Valerie and Charlene.

"This is our victim. His name was Crockett Schneider. He was the mastermind behind the biggest illegal immigrant trafficking ring in the Four Corners area. And now he's dead. He was stabbed in the chest and the murder weapon severed his aorta."

Charlene made a sour face.

"Lovely."

Valerie frowned.

"Crockett Schneider? But Colonel Tomlinson said the victim was illegal. That name...."

Charlene interrupted her.

"The Colonel didn't say he was illegal. He said the O-Line worked to curb illegals crossing the border. He never said anything about the victim."

Dan smiled and nodded.

"I knew you two would be onto this case like a pair of rabid pit bulls. Schneider wasn't illegal. He was true blue American."

"Then what was he doing running illegals across the border?" Valerie asked.

Dan snorted.

"He did it for the money, plain and simple. He charged them incredible amounts to smuggle them into the States. When he got caught, he would play dumb and babble away in Spanish, and everyone assumed he was illegal, too. He got deported back to Mexico a dozen times, but that was just his fancy way of getting off the hook so he could turn around and do it all over again. He must have pulled that trick twenty times."

"Clever," Charlene exclaimed.

"If he did it so many times," Valerie asked, "didn't your team know better? Why didn't they keep him here?"

"That's the problem," Dan replied.

"Our team knew about him and his little game, but it wasn't always us that arrested him. We put the word out to as many other agencies as we could not to deport him, but the information didn't always filter through. More than once, the arresting officers didn't even bother to check this mug shot against the characters they found in the back of the truck. They heard a bunch of Spanish and deported everyone with no questions asked. It happens all the time. The most wanted outlaws on our list can get off scot free by pretending to be illegals who don't speak English."

Dan's expression was grim, and the frustration he felt about the situation was obvious.

"Is that what happened this time?" Valerie asked. "Did he escape from a deportation transport?"

"This time was different," Dan replied.

"This time, two of our team arrested Schneider with a truckload of illegals crossing the border near Laredo. They knew what they had, and they weren't taking him back to Mexico—no way! They were taking him to San Antonio where they had a grand jury all lined up. They were going to roll into town and have Schneider put away within hours."

Charlene waved both hands back and forth.

"Now just hold on there, Cochise. This doesn't make sense at all. The Colonel said he was killed in Flagstaff. You're telling me he was being transported from Laredo to San Antonio. Flagstaff is nowhere near that route. He would have had to travel all the way across West Texas, and then across New Mexico, and then across half of Arizona to get to Flagstaff. That makes no sense."

Dan laughed out loud.

"This is what I love about working with you two. Nothing gets past you."

"So are you telling us he got all the way across the American Southwest before he was murdered?" Valerie asked.

"That's exactly what I'm telling you," Dan replied. "But he didn't run there on foot. He drove there in a car that was waiting for him near Dilley. The O-Liners who arrested him stopped at a roadside gas station to fuel up, and when one of the agents lifted the hood to check the oil and water, Schneider made a break for it. He ran to a car parked nearby. He pulled the keys out of his pocket, turned the ignition, and drove away."

Valerie and Charlene stared at him.

"Just like that?" Charlene gasped.

"Just like that," Dan replied.

"Did the agents give chase?" Valerie asked.

"They started to," Dan told her. "But they hadn't filled up their gas tank. They didn't make it more than thirty miles before they ran out of gas, and Schneider rode off into the sunset."

"He rode off into the sunset to Flagstaff, where he was murdered," Charlene added.

Dan laughed. "Do you want to know the weirdest thing?"

"Do you mean weirder than him having the key to the car in his pocket when he was in Federal custody?" Valerie asked. "Or weirder than the car waiting at a place neither he nor anyone else could have known the agents were going to stop?"

"Weirder than that," Dan replied.

"Let's hear it," Charlene told him.

"The weirdest thing," Dan replied, "is that all our evidence suggests he knew he was going to be murdered in Flagstaff."

Valerie frowned. "How do you figure? Why would he go there if he knew?"

Dan opened the file and took out several sheets of paper.

"Take a look. We tracked several members of his organization, and we found out one of his most trusted lieutenants, a certain Emilio Donnelly, turned traitor and switched to a rival organization about three months ago. He joined The Machos."

"The Machos," Charlene repeated. "That's the most dangerous gang operating across the border."

Valerie nodded.

"Not only that, but they've sworn to kill any Gringos they catch transporting illegals into the country. They believe Gringos can't be trusted and they're all working for the Federals."

"But Donnelly is a Gringo name," Charlene pointed out. "Why would a Gringo join an anti-Gringo gang?"

"He's half Gringo and half Mexican," Dan replied. "He contacted The Machos three months ago behind Schneider's back. If he joined, he would have to prove himself by killing Schneider."

"But Schneider must have known Donnelly would come after him and try to kill him," Valerie pointed out. "You can't tell me you found out Donnelly contacted The Machos but Schneider didn't know."

Dan nodded.

"That's what I'm trying to tell you. We intercepted a message, which was sent to one of Schneider's contacts in Juarez, telling him to meet Donnelly at a motel in Flagstaff. In fact, Schneider's getaway car was listed with a rental company in San Antonio under the name Mark Everest, which is one of Donnelly's known aliases. Donnelly arranged the getaway car for him, and Schneider planned to meet him at the motel to pay him for his service or something like that."

Charlene puffed out her cheeks. "Crikey! That's a lot to swallow in one mouthful."

"You're telling me," Valerie exclaimed.

Dan stood up and closed the file.

"You two are coming with me to Texas."

"What's there?" Valerie asked. "Donnelly will be long gone."

"He's in custody in San Antonio right now," Dan replied. "Our team busted one of his illegal trafficking compounds near Sedona. We're going to interview him first before someone decides to rid the world of his pesky ways. After that, we'll go to Flagstaff to check out the motel where Schneider was killed."

Valerie followed him to the door.

"This is going to be an expensive case. First, we have to drive from Denver to San Antonio, then back to Flagstaff, then who knows where."

"We're not driving," Dan told her. "We're flying."

Valerie stopped in her tracks.

"Flying?"

"Yeah, flying," he replied. "You know, in a plane."

She stared at him.

"Plane?"

Dan laughed out loud.

"The O-Line has a plane waiting at the airport. That's how I got here from Phoenix. I didn't drive here in my beat-up old Toyota Corolla."

"What Corolla?" Valerie asked. "You rolled up to EdenCloud in a Cadillac with leather seats. You never drove any Corolla. Who are you trying to kid?"

Dan smiled down at her. A flush of happiness colored his cheeks.

"That was a rental, but you're right. I don't drive a Corolla."

"What do you drive?" Valerie asked.

He dropped his voice to a whisper.

"I drive a vintage Landcruiser."

Valerie snorted. "I should have known."

"But I have another Cadillac rented while I'm in Denver. Come down to the parking garage with me. I'll give you a ride to the airport."

"Hang on a minute." Valerie ducked into her office and grabbed a blue shoulder bag from under her desk.

Dan raised his eyebrows.

"What's that — your make-up case?"

Valerie slapped him on the arm.

"No, fool. It's my overnight bag for when random Federal agents blow in and want to whisk me across the country with no notice whatsoever. It's got an extra toothbrush and toothpaste, a hair brush, nail clippers, a clean pair of underwear, that sort of thing."

Dan raised his eyebrows.

"You carry underwear around with you on murder cases?"

Charlene stuck her head between them.

"Are you two finished? Can we get going now?"

Valerie turned bright red and walked away. Dan and Charlene followed. Over her shoulder, Valerie overheard them talking.

"I never met an agent like Valerie before. She's full of surprises."

"You don't know the half of it," Charlene shot back. "Do you know what she did the other day? She told Jeff Everson...."

"Who's Jeff Everson?" Dan asked.

Valerie whirled around.

"Do you mind? I thought we were on our way to the airport."

Dan's eyes widened.

"We're just making small talk. There's nothing more to say about the case until we get to San Antonio."

Valerie turned away. She stormed into the stairwell and ran down the steps two at a time, all the way to the parking garage. She couldn't stand around and listen to anything Charlene told Dan about Jeff Everson. Leave it to Charlene to blow the lid clean off that can of worms.

Chapter 2

A flight attendant set two dewy champagne glasses on Valerie's tray table. Valerie glanced up.

"I don't want two."

The flight attendant only smiled and disappeared. A moment later, Dan slid into the seat next to her. He picked up a glass and touched it to Valerie's.

"Here's to another successful working partnership."

Valerie studied him.

"You planned this whole thing, didn't you?"

He choked on his champagne. "Valerie! How can you accuse me of conspiring to benefit from the Federal law enforcement system? The O-Line had a case we couldn't tackle alone, so I suggested to my superior officer that we contact the Strikeforce Team for reinforcements. I told my team about the work you did at EdenCloud, and they agreed to engage your services to help me track down Schneider's killer. That's all I did. I swear it."

He sipped his champagne, but his eyes never left Valerie's face. She scrutinized him more closely. Was he joking or not? She sighed and took another sip of her drink.

"You O-Liners sure know how to travel, don't you?"

Dan shrugged.

"Like you said, it would be too expensive to drive to investigate a case that spans most of the Western US. It would take too long, and we have to move quickly. We can't take regular domestic airline flights. We would spend half our lives waiting around in airports."

"Yeah, but still." Valerie waved her hands at the plush seats, the wide spaces between the seats, and the champagne flutes in their hands. "

I'd be surprised if the richest celebrities travel in this kind of style. It's a bit... you know... excessive for a taxpayer funded service."

"The O-Line isn't taxpayer funded," he told her.

Valerie stared at him.

"It isn't?"

He shook his head.

"We pay for everything out of funds confiscated from drug smugglers and people traffickers working across the border. The O-Line is the one agency in the country that doesn't cost the taxpayers a cent, and we're the ones doing the most to protect this country from foreign invasion."

"That's what Colonel Tomlinson said," Valerie replied. "But if you're protecting the country from invasion, shouldn't you be calling yourselves the D-Line?"

Dan didn't laugh at the joke.

"We don't sit back and wait for the enemy to strike. We send operatives into enemy territory to stop them before they start. We're the unsung heroes in the battle to protect this land from the rising tide of alien encroachment."

Valerie's jaw dropped.

"You're serious! Have you done that? Have you gone across the border to hit hostile elements who try to breach our border?"

He nodded, and his soft brown eyes glittered.

"Many times. I've penetrated some of the most dangerous jungle in Mexico to find the hideouts of illegal traffickers, and I've blown their operations to kingdom come. I've executed dozens of hits on known smugglers who brought thousands of illegals into our country. Now I supervise others doing the same thing. I train them in tactical battle skills, guerrilla warfare and weapons. I have ten operatives across the border as we speak."

Valerie shook her head.

"Why didn't you tell me any of this at EdenCloud? You never let on that you were law enforcement, too, and I never even heard of the O-Line until today. Heck, not even the famous Charlene Brockworth has heard of it."

Dan smiled.

"We like to keep a low profile. We couldn't function if everybody knew about us and wanted to monitor our activities. We prefer to remain anonymous."

"There's anonymous," she replied, "and then there's anonymous."

"Not even our enemies know we exist," he declared. "If they don't know we exist, they can't counter us. They don't know we're onto them until we strike, and when we do, they never know what hit them. One minute, they're counting their gold in their mountain hideouts. The next minute they're floating on a cloud explaining their life story to Saint Peter and wondering where it all went wrong. If Saint Peter explains to them about the O-Line at that point, I won't take issue with him."

"You're really the Men in Black," Valerie exclaimed. "You're not going to wipe our memories after we wrap up this case, are you?"

He leaned over and cradled her chin in his hand.

"I couldn't do that. I couldn't do anything that would make you forget about me."

Valerie's heart fluttered.

"Dan, I...."

He shook his head.

"Don't say it. I've been waiting for a chance to get back in touch with you. The Strikeforce Team isn't the easiest to penetrate either, you know. Can you forgive me for using this case to get close to you?"

"It isn't that," Valerie explained. "You know I'm happy to see you again. I just...."

He bent down and kissed her. Champagne sparkled on his lips.

"You're the best agent I ever met, Valerie. I can't think of anyone I would rather work with on this case. I hope this is the beginning of you and me spending a lot more time together, and I don't mean on murder cases."

Before she could answer, he covered her mouth with his lips again. She let herself melt into his kiss, and his intoxicating breath sent her head spinning.

Then he leaned back with a satisfied smile, got up, and walked away.

In the space he left behind, Valerie noticed Charlene watching her from across the aisle. Charlene shook her head and sipped her champagne.

"What?" Valerie asked.

"When are you gonna learn?" Charlene asked.

Valerie shifted in her seat.

"I don't know what you're talking about."

"I'm talking about the way you always hook up with every guy that crosses your path," Charlene replied.

Valerie slouched in her seat and humphed.

"I do *not* hook up with every guy that crosses my path."

Charlene counted off on her fingers. "You hooked up with Jeff at the Mackenzie Lodge. Then you hooked up with Dan Henderson at EdenCloud. Then you got back with Jeff in Denver, and now you're making the moves on Dan again."

"That's two guys," Valerie pointed out. "I do not hook up with every guy that crosses my path, and I am not making the moves on Dan. If you've been sitting there eavesdropping on our conversation, you should know he's the one making the moves on me, not the other way around."

"What are you going to do when Jeff gets back?" Charlene asked. "What are you going to tell him about how you've been cozying up to Dan on this job?"

Valerie looked the other way.

"Maybe Jeff won't get back until we finish this job. Maybe he'll never find out about Dan."

Charlene stared at her across the aisle. Then she snorted and shook her head again.

"I don't understand you at all. I thought you and Jeff were getting serious."

"What gave you that idea?" Valerie asked.

"You spend all your time together," Charlene replied. "You eat together, you discuss your cases together, you go out together in your free time. You leave work together and you come into the office together in the morning. You can't tell me you two aren't heading toward something serious."

Valerie shrugged.

"We never talked about it. We're working together. That's all."

"That is definitely not all," Charlene shot back. "Do you think every agent in the Strikeforce penthouse suite doesn't know you two spend every night together?"

Valerie's mouth fell open. "What?"

Charlene pursed her lips.

"You must think we're all really stupid. You spend just about every night in Jeff's room. You don't have to play innocent."

Valerie swallowed and turned away. What could she say?

"What are you going to tell Dan about Jeff?" Charlene held up her hand. "Don't even think about telling me you plan to keep him in the dark. You have to tell them about each other," she insisted.

"If you don't consider your relationship with Jeff serious, you better make that perfectly clear to him before you do anything with Dan, because I'll bet cold hard cash he considers his relationship with you serious. So if you do anything with Dan, you'll be cheating on Jeff. Is that what you want to do?"

Valerie stared at her.

"What are you—the moral police?"

Charlene shrugged.

"I'm just saying you're treading on thin ice here, girl."

Chapter 3

The plane's wheels screeched on the tarmac, and the plane taxied to the far end of the runway. It didn't go near the main terminal, though. It cruised to a hangar in the distant back corner of the airport, where it stopped. The engine whined to a standstill. The flight attendant opened the door and let down the stairs.

"Welcome to San Antonio."

Valerie and Charlene put their tray tables away and stood up. No one had told them to put their tray tables away or buckle their seat belts to prepare for landing. None of those pesky rules and regulations had marred the tranquility of the flight. Valerie sighed and stretched. This was the most relaxing flight she'd ever taken in her life.

Dan waved down at the ground.

"Whenever you're ready."

Valerie and Charlene descended the stairs. The sticky humid air of Texas in summer clutched at Valerie's throat. Dan gestured to an unmarked black sedan waiting for them nearby.

"Here's our car."

Valerie's head whipped around.

"This?"

She scrutinized the car. It was a BMW, a turbo, but something was missing.

She looked closer. Then she realized why it looked so strange. It had no license plate.

Dan popped the driver's door. The keys were in the ignition.

"Get in."

Valerie hesitated.

"Where did this car come from?"

"The O-Line arranges all this sort of thing," he replied. "Now get in. The day's half over, and we have to interview Donnelly before the lock-up closes for the afternoon."

He slammed the driver's door, and the car roared to life.

Valerie bent her head toward Charlene.

"And I thought the Strikeforce Team was elite."

"These O-Liners are in a league of their own," Charlene replied. "It must be nice not to have to arrange your own rental cars."

"This car is no rental," Valerie countered. "This is something else entirely. I wouldn't be surprised if these O-Liners have diplomatic immunity or something similar."

"They're law enforcement," Charlene pointed out. "How can they have immunity?"

"They're not law enforcement," Valerie replied. "They aren't military, and they aren't intelligence. They're unique."

Charlene took the front passenger seat and Valerie climbed into the back seat. Why did she do that? Why did she hesitate to sit next to Dan?

Actually, she hadn't hesitated to sit next to him. She had hesitated to sit next to him in front of Charlene. Charlene didn't approve of her and Dan.

Then again, there was no her and Dan — at least, there shouldn't be. Valerie had spent months of careful manipulation on convincing Charlene that her relationship with Jeff Everson was legitimate and wouldn't damage the Strikeforce Team. And now she found out that Charlene — and probably the rest of the team, too — knew all about their supposedly clandestine rendezvous in the penthouse suite at night. What else did they know?

And yet she couldn't blame Charlene for disapproving. What was she thinking, getting mixed up with one man while she was developing a relationship with another? What was she — some kind of tramp? She ought to have her head examined.

Charlene was right. She would have to tell Dan about Jeff before their relationship went any further. And she would have to tell Jeff about Dan when he came back. He had a right to know what went on between them in his absence. That was the least she could do for him after the time they'd spent together.

She cringed at the thought of talking to either man about the other.

She'd never admired anyone more than these two men. She couldn't stand the thought of pushing either of them away. Both of them possessed more integrity than a boatload of Boy Scouts. They would both want her for themselves, and they wouldn't stand anyone else laying claim to her.

The BMW glided through the busy streets of San Antonio. Valerie gazed through the window at nothing, absorbed in her own thoughts, until she noticed where they were.

"Where are you going? This isn't the way into town."

"We're not going into town," Dan replied. "We're going to Fort Sam Houston."

Valerie's head whipped around.

"What? I thought you said Donnelly was in custody."

"He's in Federal custody," Dan corrected her. "He's in a maximum security holding facility on the military base. We couldn't run the risk of him escaping from the police."

Charlene spoke up.

"I guess you're taking extra precautions after Schneider gave you the slip."

Dan turned off the expressway.

"You bet we are."

He handed his ID card to the guard at the gate, who waved them through without even checking his credentials. Valerie's head swam. These O-Liners must be the top tier of the law enforcement community. And she'd never guessed.

When she'd comforted Dan at EdenCloud and solved the mystery of his father's murder, she'd never suspected that he was sizing her up all along.

What did he see when he watched her mucking around, questioning suspects, making a joke out of the whole case? What must he be thinking now? She was completely out of her depth in his world. Even the great Charlene Brockworth was out of her depth in his world.

Dan parked in front of a Quonset hut painted plain grey with no numbers or identifying markings on the outside. Before opening the car door, he handed Valerie and Charlene photo ID cards. Each card consisted of nothing but a stock image of each of them with a bar code underneath.

"Put those on, and no one will ask any questions."

He strode across the parking lot so fast Valerie and Charlene had to trot to keep up with him. Even now, his shoulders stood out – somehow seeming broader and more intimidating than they ever had at EdenCloud. A flash of lightning illuminated his face, and he didn't hesitate when he opened the door and stepped inside the building.

A corporal in fatigues guarded the door, with a rifle resting on the floor at his side. He snapped to attention when Dan appeared. He didn't look at Valerie or Charlene or check their IDs. Dan walked right past him, and down a long hall lined with doors on either side. He continued all the way to the far end of the building before he stopped.

He unclipped his ID card from his lapel and scanned the bar code on an electronic pad next to the door knob.

A lock clicked, and the three investigators stepped inside.

A plate of bulletproof glass partitioned the room. On the other side, a shaggy man in bright orange overalls sat on a plain metal cot. Nothing else but a toilet bowl and sink occupied the room. Solid concrete walls surrounded the man on every side, except for the glass. He looked up when the investigators entered. Then he burst into hysterical laughter.

"Well, if it isn't good old Captain Dan. I wondered when I'd see you again."

"Hello there, Emilio," Dan replied. "I hope you're comfortable here."

Donnelly waved his hand to one side.

"Who could be anything but comfortable in a place like this? I have everything I could ever want. I have all the booze I can drink, and all the dope I can smoke, and all the video games I could want to play. I get to watch TV all day long, and I have these two lovely ladies come to visit me. What more could I ask for?"

The benign smile evaporated from Dan's face. "These two lovely ladies are Federal agents investigating Crockett Schneider's murder. I'll thank you to treat them with respect."

Donnelly cocked his head to one side.

"*They're* investigating Schneider's death? Not likely. *You're* investigating Schneider's death, and you don't need any lovely ladies to help you, either. Is one of them your girlfriend? Maybe both of them are your girlfriends. Maybe you brought them down here to impress them with what a big man you are."

Valerie's cheeks burst into flame, but Dan kept his voice steady.

"You can believe what you want to believe. We're not here to impress you. We're here to ask you some questions about Schneider."

"Ask me anything you want."

Donnelly settled back on his cot.

"You met with him at the Lamplighter Motel in Flagstaff before he died," Dan began.

Donnelly's head spun around.

"Who told you that?"

"You rented the car Schneider used to escape the last time he was captured," Dan pointed out. "You rented the car in San Antonio and planted it near Dilley so Schneider could give us the slip. He drove all the way to Flagstaff, where he met you at the hotel. You killed him there."

Donnelly shook his head.

"If you believe that, what are you doing here questioning me about it? You must not be certain that I killed him. If you were certain, you would add the murder charge to the case against me. You wouldn't bring your girlfriends here to ask questions about it."

Dan shrugged. "But you rented the car. You admit that, don't you?"

Donnelly turned away. "What if I did? That doesn't mean I killed him."

"Did you meet him at his motel room before he died?" Dan asked.

Donnelly fixed him with a fierce glare.

"Are you asking me or telling me?"

"Are you asking me or telling me?" Dan repeated. "We have a report from the motel clerk that you visited Schneider's room before he died."

"I didn't," Donnelly muttered.

"You didn't, but Mark Everest did," Dan replied.

Donnelly threw up his hands. He launched himself off the cot and paced around the room.

"All right. All right. I rented the car, and I planted it in our usual spot near Dilley. There. I said it."

"How did you manage to get the agents to stop at your usual spot to fuel up?" Dan asked.

Donnelly snorted. "You're not as bright as you think, Captain Dan. That gas station is the only spot on the road to fill up. The agents wouldn't have a choice but to stop there if they wanted to get to San Antonio in one piece."

"Then how did you get the keys to him?" Dan asked. "He must have had the keys in his pocket when the agents took him into custody."

Donnelly shook his head. "I don't know who told you that. He never had the keys in his pocket."

"That's what the agents reported when he escaped," Dan told him.

Donnelly choked with laughter.

"They spun you a yarn to get themselves off the hook. The keys were in the ignition, and I left a sign in the window to show Schneider which car was his. That's all. He ran to the car, got in, and drove away."

"He drove all the way to Flagstaff," Dan added, "where you met him and killed him."

"We met in Flagstaff," Donnelly replied. "But I give you my word of honor he was alive when I left him."

Dan raised one eyebrow.

"Your word of honor?"

Donnelly grumbled something under his breath. Then he waved his fist at Dan.

"You people think you're so much better than us," he started. "You think you can waltz in here and insult me. Well, I have my own honor," he continued, "and I tell you, on my mother's grave, if I killed Crockett Schneider, I would admit it. I never wanted the guy dead. I'm already going away for life. I've got nothing to lose by lying about it."

Dan chuckled. "You can't fool me, Emilio. Your mother is alive and well and living in Fresno."

Donnelly stared at him. Then he sank back down on his cot.

"Leave me alone, man. You already put me away for good. Leave me to rot in peace."

Dan gazed down at him. "Do you really expect me to believe you didn't kill Schneider to get into The Machos?"

Donnelly snorted, but he didn't look up.

"I couldn't get into the Machos. They wouldn't take me, no matter what I did."

Dan nodded. "Let me guess. You've got too much Gringo blood."

Donnelly winced and turned his head even farther away.

"I didn't kill him, man. You can believe what you want to believe, but if you investigate, you'll find out I'm telling the truth."

"Do you know who did kill him?" Dan asked.

Donnelly stole a sidelong glance at him. "You wouldn't believe me if I told you."

"Try me," Dan replied.

Donnelly shook his head. "I can't."

"But you know who did it, don't you?" Dan asked. "You must know who met Schneider in Flagstaff after you left him."

Donnelly nodded. "He said he was meeting another operator in the trade. He wanted me to leave right away. He gave me the money to pay for the car and the other expenses of getting him out of Texas. Then he told me to take a hike."

"Who was he meeting?" Dan asked.

Donnelly shrank down on his cot. He spoke in a voice so soft they could barely hear him. "You'll see."

Dan turned away and motioned Valerie and Charlene out of the room.

Chapter 4

The door slammed and silence filled the hall. Valerie turned to Dan.

"Do you believe him?"

Dan shrugged.

"Why not? If he really killed Schneider to get into The Machos, he would be crowing to high heaven about it."

"You sounded pretty certain Donnelly killed Schneider back in Denver," Valerie pointed out. "You said you intercepted a message for Donnelly to meet Schneider at the motel, and that Schneider knew Donnelly had betrayed him by joining The Machos."

Dan strode down the hall.

"We got a message, but I suppose Donnelly only tried to join The Machos. They wouldn't take him. His mother is white, and they only take men with pure Mexican blood."

"Or," Charlene countered, "he really did join The Machos and he's lying about killing Schneider."

Dan shook his head.

"The Machos is a brutal gang. They mark their members for life so they can never join any other group. Didn't you notice Donnelly's feet?"

"What about them?" Valerie asked. "They looked normal to me."

"That's what I mean," Dan replied. "The Machos runs their new members through a torturous hazing process. They remove the outer two toenails from their members' feet, and the new member has to endure the pain without screaming. Donnelly had all his toenails."

"They could have regrown," Valerie pointed out.

"They don't grow back," Dan replied. "They treat the nail bed with phenol to ensure other gangs can identify the initiate later on. That's their way of ensuring loyalty in their members."

Valerie shook her head and turned away.

"This is nuts."

"He didn't join The Machos," Dan went on, "so he had no reason to kill Schneider. Let's get back to the airport and get over to Flagstaff. We have to find out who Schneider met before he died."

"How can you be sure Donnelly isn't just trying to get you off his case?" Valerie asked. "He doesn't like you very much."

"He hates me," Dan snorted. "He'll hate me for the rest of his life, now that I'm putting him away."

"You said the O-Line busted one of their trafficking compounds," Valerie remarked.

Dan nodded.

"He and three accomplices had hundreds of illegal women and children imprisoned there, and they were selling them to Chinese body smugglers for extraordinary amounts of money. Schneider would bring these people over the border in trucks and vans, and in the trunks of cars, and drop them off at this compound. They never saw the light of day again until they got to China."

Valerie shuddered.

"How awful."

"You should have seen the conditions they kept these people in," Dan went on. "I spent months tracking them with two teams of agents. We started in the Sonoran mountains and tracked them all the way here before we busted the whole ring. Only Schneider got away."

"How did Donnelly arrange the rental and meet Schneider in Flagstaff before he was arrested?" Valerie asked.

"Schneider was arrested in Laredo on May 4th," Dan replied. "According to our records, Donnelly met Schneider at the Lamplighter on May 6th. They must have had the rendezvous point agreed upon ahead of time, or maybe Donnelly left a note in the rental car. Schneider was killed no more than an hour after the motel clerk reported him meeting Donnelly there. We busted the compound a week later on May 13th. That gives Donnelly more than enough time to get from Flagstaff to Sedona."

"Where are the other men you arrested?" Valerie asked.

Dan jerked his thumb back down the hall in the direction they'd come.

"They're all here. None of them is going anywhere."

Valerie stared down that empty hall. Silence reigned through the building. The guard at the door stood ramrod straight and didn't blink. Two or three dozen doors stood on either side of the hall, with a man behind each one — a man at the end of his useful life. Each one would spend the rest of his days in a place just like this. The criminals the O-Line put away never came back.

Dan touched her arm.

"Are you coming?"

Valerie sighed and turned to follow him and Charlene out of the building. But at that moment, a hail of gunfire rang through the building. The guard jumped a foot into the air and whipped his rifle up to his shoulder just as a door at the far end of the hall burst open.

Another door flew open, and two men ran into the hall. They both carried rifles, and pistols stuck out of their belts. Dan whirled around.

"What in the...."

The guard took aim and got off one shot before the prisoners knelt down in the middle of the hall and fired back. One bullet hit the guard in the shoulder, and he went down.

Dan yanked his pistol out from under his jacket, and Valerie clawed her own weapon out of its holster behind her back.

Charlene rushed back into the room from outside, but the next moment, they all hit the floor. A maelstrom of gunfire rattled around their heads, and they scrambled for cover behind the guard's desk.

Another three doors burst open, then another two. In front of their eyes, prisoners flooded into the hall, bristling with weapons. Dan peeked over the desk, and the prisoners rained dozens of bullets at him. He crouched behind the desk with his gun poised to shoot.

"How are they getting out of their cells?"

Valerie shouted back over the din.

"Where did they get the weapons? That's what I'd like to know."

Dan glanced around.

"We have to get out of here. They outnumber us by two to one."

"How are we going to get out?" Valerie asked. "We can't get to the door without breaking our cover."

Dan stole another glance at the prisoners.

"We have to do something. They're almost on top of us."

Valerie took a look.

"We have to stop them advancing any further. If they get to the guard, they'll kill him." She reared up behind the desk. "Cover me."

Dan bellowed back. "What?"

Valerie didn't wait to answer him. She jumped to her feet and fired at the prisoners. At the same moment, Dan rose to his feet at her side, and together they hammered the prisoners with shot after shot. The prisoners paused in their advance. At least they hadn't reached the guard yet. Valerie couldn't hope for much more than to stop them from killing him.

The guard caught sight of Dan and Valerie and heard the gunshots exploding over his head and pinging against the far wall. He roused himself and rolled over with a pained grunt. His blood smeared the floor, and sweat stood out on his pale skin. He clawed at the slick tile floor to get onto his hands and knees. He slipped in his own blood and fell. He fought his way to the desk, and with his last shred of strength, he launched himself onto his knees with his hand outstretched. He slammed his hand against a red button on the wall and collapsed back onto his face on the floor.

A deafening siren screeched through the building. It echoed across the base. Valerie peered down at the guard. He lay with his eyes closed and cradled his head on his arm. She couldn't see him breathing, but a contented smile spread over his face.

He'd done it. He'd sounded the alarm, and the cavalry would be coming soon.

The prisoners stopped in their tracks at the sound of the siren and looked at Donnelly for direction. He listened to the noise. Then he waved his pistol in the air.

"Come on. Let's go."

The prisoners started forward again, and Donnelly fired at the investigators behind the desk.

His friends copied him, and one bullet ripped through the plywood desk. Splinters flew up into Valerie's face, and she covered her face with her arm to protect her eyes.

Another sally of bullets crashed through the building. She took a step back to get away from them, but she tripped over Charlene's foot and pitched headlong onto the floor. She still held her arm in front of her face, so she didn't see where she was until she hit the ground. When she opened her eyes, she stared up at Donnelly and his friends charging straight for her. She was lying across the middle of the hall with nothing in the world to protect her from the enemy.

Dan spotted her and blasted away at the prisoners with his pistol, but they wouldn't stop now. They paid no attention to him and pushed forward. In a matter of seconds, they would be on top of Valerie, and they would shoot her where she lay along with the injured guard.

Dan read the situation in an instant, and he rocketed out from behind the desk. He fired at the prisoners as he ran and dove headfirst onto the floor in front of Valerie. He missed his mark and landed on top of her. His weight crushed her into the floor, but his body protected her from the flying bullets.

He emptied his clip at Donnelly. Then he pulled a spare from his holster and popped off that one, too.

Valerie hid under the protective bulk of his body and listened to the metallic snap of his weapon sliding open and staying open. His gun was empty, and he had nothing left to fill it with. Valerie was out of bullets, and Charlene's weapon fell silent, too.

They were defenseless before these criminals bent on escape. The guard's pistol was across the room, but even that didn't have enough bullets in it to save them now.

A deadly silence fell over the building, and Valerie closed her eyes. Dan bent his head, and his face nestled into the soft corner of her neck. There was nothing left to do but wait for death. At least she would die with him.

The prisoners saw their chance and charged forward with their weapons ready for the slaughter. But before they could take more than a few steps, the door crashed open and a squad of MPs charged into the building. They formed ranks and assaulted the prisoners with continuous blasts of rifle fire. A few prisoners made a feeble attempt to fight back, but they realized, before long, that it was hopeless. They dropped their weapons and raised their arms above their heads.

The tide turned after that. It turned so fast that Valerie almost couldn't comprehend it. The MPs herded the prisoners back into their cells. The sergeant in charge stationed two MPs outside every cell. Then he returned to Dan where he bent over a stretcher and squeezed the guard's hand.

"You'll be all right now." Paramedics surrounded the prostrate figure and hung an IV from his arm.

The guard gasped for breath and struggled to sit up. He grabbed Dan's hand.

"Thank you, Sir. You saved my life."

"Save your breath, soldier." Dan pushed him back down. "They'll take you to the sick bay and patch you up. You did your duty, so you can rest easy now."

The guard gave him a weak nod and sank back onto the stretcher. The medics picked him up and ferried him out of the building.

The sergeant saluted Dan and pointed down the hall.

"If you're ready to make an inspection of the lock-up, Sir, we'll try to locate the equipment they used to override the door locks."

"I don't have time to inspect the lock-up," Dan replied. "I'm on my way to Flagstaff to finish my investigation. Toss their cells and see what you find, but I don't like your chances."

Valerie came to his side.

"How do you think they opened their doors?"

"They had help from the outside," Dan replied. "Someone gave them those weapons, and they haven't seen another human soul besides their lawyers since they got here. The locks must have been hacked electronically. Someone broke into the base mainframe and overrode the security codes."

"What can you do about that?" Valerie asked.

Dan nodded to the sergeant.

"That's base business now. Us hanging around won't solve that problem. They'll have to search their computer programs and set up new layers of security. In the meantime, we have a case to investigate."

He waved toward the door and ushered Valerie and Charlene back outside. The blazing sunshine sizzled on Valerie's skin.

The deadly reality of the lock-up building faded into another dimension.

Chapter 5

Dan drove them back to the airport in silence. They found the plane with its engine whining and the chocks removed from its wheels. Dan parked the Beamer in the same place he'd found it and slammed the door.

"What will happen to the car?" Valerie asked.

Dan shrugged.

"The team will pick it up later."

"How did the pilot know we were coming?" she asked.

Dan laughed.

"The guard at the base must have sent him a message."

Valerie peered at his face, but he only laughed down at her. What a joke that was!

They climbed the air stairs and took their seats, and the plane took off.

Valerie watched the crimson streaks of sunset spread over the western horizon. The plane banked and climbed through the clouds, and Valerie gazed down at the sun dropping behind the distant mountains. In a moment, the mountains fell away underneath them, and only the wide expanse of desert stretched out below them.

The clouds faded from crimson to gold to green, and then deepened into midnight blue. Stars twinkled in the east, even as the sun gasped its last breath in the west. Valerie sighed. A thousand thoughts fought for real estate in her mind, but the deafening thunder of gunfire dominated her consciousness. She ought to concentrate on solving this case, but nothing made sense anymore.

Dan walked back from the front cabin, and Valerie caught snatches of conversation between him and Charlene farther up the plane. What were they talking about without her present? She jumped out of her seat and strode up the aisle.

They sat on either side of a table in the mid-cabin. Dan pointed to a sheet of paper spread out on the surface between them.

"Right here."

"And where were the conspirators found?" Charlene asked.

Dan slid his finger farther along the page.

"Here. They had a big computer set-up to track every one of their transports, and they microchipped every person they transported. Once they got hold of you, you weren't going anywhere until they decided to let you go."

"What are you talking about?" Valerie asked.

Dan smiled up at her.

"Charlene wanted to know more about the compound where I arrested Donnelly and his men."

"What for?" Valerie asked. "That's not material to this case."

"Schneider was captured transporting illegals to this compound," Charlene told her.

"He and Donnelly ran this operation together. We need to know everything about their business."

Valerie frowned. Dan waved her to a seat near him.

"Why don't you join us? You should be hearing this, too. It could lead us to the person who killed Schneider."

Valerie gazed down at the diagram in front of them. How easy it would be to sit down in that chair and talk over the case without a care in the world.

But she couldn't. Why? Why did she have to torture herself like this? Why did she have to create problems out of nothing?

She shook her head.

"I have to go to the bathroom."

She walked away up the aisle. The plane swayed under her, and she kept her balance by alternating her hands from one seat to the next. She found the bathroom door next to the galley at the front of the plane. The flight attendant smiled at her between setting champagne flutes on a tray.

Valerie smiled back and turned away. Was that flight attendant a member of the O-Line, too? Did she cross the border to hit the enemies of the United States in their Sonoran mountain hideouts? What had that flight attendant seen in the time she'd been working on this plane? Valerie could only imagine.

Valerie pushed her way into the bathroom—and stopped.

Why was she surprised at what she found? This was no chemical-smelling cubicle with urine stains on the floor and a black hole into the atmosphere.

Pristine white porcelain fixtures lined the walls, and she actually had to take four steps across a tiled floor to reach the stall. A pleasant warm glow radiated up from the floor. Fresh white towels hung next to the sink, and golden light reflected off the mirror to fill the room. The toilet had a bidet button next to the flushing mechanism, and the toilet paper was Charmin UltraSoft.

Valerie leaned over the sink and ran the water. It ran hot instantly, with no delay. She splashed water on her face and rubbed her eyes. They would land in Flagstaff in an hour at the most. When would they get some sleep? They couldn't go banging on the motel owner's door to ask about Crockett Schneider — at least not until morning.

Valerie dried her face and went out. Dan met her at the door.

"Are you all right?"

Of course the flight attendant had disappeared. Valerie dropped her eyes and nodded.

"I guess I'm just tired."

"We'll get a hotel room in Flagstaff and spend the night before we visit Schneider's motel," he told her.

Valerie's head shot up.

"Don't tell me the O-Line has its own hotels in every city."

"Of course we don't," he replied. "We'll stay at the Hyatt."

Valerie stared at him. Then she smiled.

"Sorry. I shouldn't be so defensive. I still haven't had a chance to thank you for saving my life back there."

"I would gladly give my life for you, Valerie. You know how I feel about you."

He lifted her chin until she looked right into his eyes. She tried to pull away, but he wouldn't let her go.

"Why are you so touchy?"

Valerie took a deep breath.

"I have to tell you something, Dan. I should have told you a long time ago, but..."

"A long time ago when?" he asked. "We only just met again for the first time a few hours ago. When would you tell me?"

Valerie shifted from one foot to the other.

"Don't change the subject. I have to tell you something. I don't want to, but I have to."

"So tell me."

"I've been seeing somebody," she told him. "I spent some time with him before I met you at EdenCloud. It was just a very brief sort of thing..."

"A brief sort of fling thing, you mean?" he asked.

Valerie shrugged.

"I guess you could call it that. I met him and spent... I don't know... maybe a weekend with him. Then I left and I didn't see him again. That's when I met you, and after we wrapped up the EdenCloud case, you went back to Phoenix and I didn't see you again, either. Then he decided to move to Denver and try out for the Strikeforce Team, and he made it. We've been working together for six months now."

Dan studied her.

"The Strikeforce Team lives in a penthouse suite on top of an office building. Are you telling me you live with this guy, too?"

Valerie stared down at her toes and nodded.

"Are you in an exclusive relationship with him?" Dan asked.

Valerie looked up.

"Well, we never really had that discussion, you know. We just sort of..."

"Sort of what?" he asked.

Valerie fidgeted.

"I don't know. I guess we just sort of floated along, doing whatever."

Dan's eyes widened.

"Doing whatever?"

Valerie didn't answer.

Dan let out a long breath.

"I see. Well, I'm glad you told me."

Valerie sucked in her breath.

"I'm sorry I didn't tell you sooner."

"When would you have told me?" he asked. "Besides, if you aren't in an exclusive relationship with him, I don't see what bearing that has on us at all. It doesn't change my feelings for you, and it won't stop me from spending time with you."

"But I'll have to tell him about you, too," Valerie told him. "I'll have to tell him about the time we spent at EdenCloud, and I'll have to explain to him that you still have feelings for me."

"Tell him whatever you want," Dan replied. "I won't stop trying to get close to you until you tell me you're exclusive with him."

"But don't you see..." Valerie began.

He cut her off with a wave of his hand.

"I do see, Valerie. I see that you don't owe him or me anything. You're not attached to anybody, so you're free to choose him or me."

"I don't want to choose either one of you," Valerie replied. "That's exactly what I'm telling you. I can't choose you over him or him over you."

Dan studied her with his piercing eyes. Then he bent down and kissed her. His warm breath spread through her mind, and she sank into his kiss. His arms wrapped around her and drew her into the intoxicating bliss of his presence.

Her arms wound around his neck of their own free will, and her body opened to him.

All at once, an alarm bell went off in her mind. What was she doing? This wasn't Jeff. She owed it to Jeff to stop this before it started. She pushed Dan away, and his eyes widened in surprise.

"What's wrong?"

Valerie shook her head.

"I can't do this. It isn't right."

"Oh, it's right, all right," he countered. "That's the problem, isn't it? It's so right you don't know what to do. But it's definitely right."

He stared at her another long moment, and when she didn't respond, he moved in to kiss her again. This time, Valerie caught him before he reached her. She planted both hands on his chest and pushed him back.

"No, Dan. I can't, not until I've had a chance to explain the situation to Jeff."

He didn't take his eyes off her.

"Alright, if that's the way you want it, that's the way we'll do it."

"That's the way I want it," she replied. "If the situation was reversed, you wouldn't want me messing around with another guy until you knew what was going on."

He softened. "You're right. I wouldn't. I should have known to expect something like this from you."

Valerie stiffened. "What's that supposed to mean?"

"I knew you had integrity," he replied. "I didn't know you had another guy going on, but now that I do know, I should have expected you to act with integrity. I respect that's what you're doing, so we'll just leave it at that."

Valerie broke into a grin.

"Thanks. I could kiss you for that."

Dan held up his hand.

"That's okay. I don't want to kiss you again until I know for certain you can do it with a clear conscience."

She touched his hand.

"Thanks."

Dan laughed.

"Okay. You can stop saying that now."

Valerie had to laugh, too.

"Okay." She glanced down the aisle. "So what do we do now?"

He jerked his head toward the back of the plane.

"Why don't you come sit down with me and Charlene? We're going over the details of Donnelly's arrest, and you should be in on that, too."

He escorted her back to the table, where Charlene sipped her champagne flute. Another glass sat on the table for Valerie, but she pushed it aside.

That was the last thing she needed right now. Dan spread out another sheet of paper on the table.

"And this is the route they used to transport their cargo over the border."

Chapter 6

Another unmarked black BMW waited for them on the runway in Flagstaff, and Dan drove through the silent streets to a hotel on the outskirts of town.

Valerie stared out the window, preoccupied with her own thoughts. She didn't look at anything until Charlene exclaimed,

"Hey! This isn't the Hyatt."

Dan chuckled.

"No, it isn't. It's a little lower profile. It's not a luxury resort, but we don't want to tip off the hostiles to our presence."

"What hostiles?" Charlene asked. "We're investigating a murder, not invading enemy territory."

"It's the same thing," Dan replied. "The smugglers have agents all over the Southwest. You never know who's telling who what. It's always better to stay undercover if you have the chance."

Charlene shook her head.

"I thought no one knew about the O-Line. If that's true, you don't have to worry about someone finding out what you're doing and where. You're undercover permanently."

"It always pays to be cautious." Dan popped the trunk and took out a black nylon duffel bag. He handed Valerie her travel bag.

"What's in the bag?" Charlene asked.

"All my traveling gear." He grinned at Valerie. "I never travel without being prepared."

He led them to the front desk, where the clerk handed him a key with no questions asked. He didn't even ask Dan for his name or reservation number. He said nothing at all. Dan pushed the button on the elevator, and they traveled to the third floor in silence.

Charlene stopped in front of the room door.

"Is there only one room for all three of us?"

Dan grinned and unlocked the door. Valerie followed Dan inside, where three doors branched off one big suite. He tossed his duffel bag into one of the rooms and waved his hand.

"Take your pick. I'm going to take a shower and go to bed. I'll see you in the morning."

He disappeared into his room and shut the door. A moment later, the hiss of the shower drifted into the suite. Charlene and Valerie exchanged glances. Charlene sighed.

"I guess we're not in Kansas anymore."

"What do you make of this O-Line stuff?" Valerie asked.

"Very hush-hush," Charlene replied. "What I can't figure out is why they called us in on this case. Dan could handle this on his own."

"Schneider's murder looks pretty straightforward, too," Valerie remarked. "If Donnelly didn't kill him to join The Machos, some other ambitious creep must have. The killer met Schneider and bumped him off. And they all lived happily ever after."

"Except for Donnelly and the others who lived in prison ever after," Charlene countered. "Oh, and Schneider, who didn't live any more at all."

"Dan's right about one thing, though," Valerie told her. "Schneider must have known he was meeting someone who planned to kill him."

"But Donnelly said he couldn't get into The Machos," Charlene argued. "Even if Schneider knew Donnelly went behind his back to approach The Machos, he would have known Donnelly couldn't get in. He's too white. They wouldn't accept him. So he would know Donnelly wasn't out to kill him."

"So who was?" Valerie asked. "Schneider met Donnelly to pay him back for the getaway car and the expenses of arranging his escape. Who else could he have met with at his motel?"

"Anybody," Charlene replied. "He could have met with anybody. It didn't even have to be someone connected to his murder."

Valerie threw herself down on the couch.

"I can't think about this case anymore, not until we get some more answers. I'm putting it out of my mind until tomorrow. I'm sure when we visit the motel, things will clear up."

"Let's go to bed, then," Charlene suggested. "We can't be dog tired tomorrow morning when Mr. Cloak and Dagger sounds the bugle."

Valerie shook her head.

"I'm not going to bed yet. It's only eight o'clock."

"If you're not thinking about the case," Charlene asked, "what are you staying up for? Are you going to watch TV?"

Valerie pulled her travel bag toward her.

"You know I don't watch TV. Besides, I've got too many things on my mind to work out before tomorrow."

A light came on in Charlene's face.

"Oh, I get it. You've got to sort out your personal life before you get back to Denver."

Valerie looked the other way.

"Call it what you want. I have more important things to think about than a murder case any Joe Schmo could solve with his eyes closed."

Charlene perched on the chair across from her.

"When are you going to tell Dan about Jeff?"

"I already did," Valerie replied.

Charlene stared back.

"You did? I'm surprised."

"I know you think I'm a shameless tramp," Valerie shot back.

"But I do have some integrity, you know. I wouldn't play two men off each other. I only got into this situation because I hadn't seen Jeff for a couple of months when I met Dan, and then Dan went out of my life so I got back together with Jeff. I never would have done any of it if I'd known they were both going to wind up in my life at the same time."

Charlene's shoulders slumped.

"I don't think you're a shameless tramp, Valerie. I'm impressed you told him about Jeff."

"I didn't just tell him about Jeff," Valerie went on. "I told him I couldn't do anything with him until I explained the situation to Jeff. I told him he would want the same consideration if their positions were reversed."

Charlene nodded.

"I see now. I'm sorry I judged you. I should have known you would do the right thing."

Valerie turned to her partner.

"You have to help me, Charlene. How am I going to get out of this? I've never been in a situation like this before."

"I can't help you, darling," Charlene replied. "I've never been in a situation like that before, either. From what I can tell, you just have to do what you're already doing. You have to wait until you see Jeff again and explain how you got into this. You have to tell him you never messed around with either of them while you were seeing the other, and that you had no idea you were going to be working with Dan. You can tell him you stopped it with Dan before it started until you could be forthright and honest with both of them."

"But Dan says I have to choose between them," Valerie explained. "How am I going to do that?"

"You would only have to choose between them if Dan stuck around to keep working with us." Charlene frowned. "He's not planning on working with us long-term, is he?"

"Man, I hope not!" Valerie exclaimed. "I mean, I don't hope he disappears anytime soon, but I hope this situation resolves itself pretty quick so I don't have two men vying for me."

Charlene laughed.

"Some women would enjoy this situation. This is the stuff romance novels are made of."

"No, thanks," Valerie grumbled. "Give me one man — any man — not two."

"What if Dan wants you to go work with him on the O-Line?" Charlene swept the suite with her hand. "What if he offers you all this luxury and prestige to battle our country's enemies? Would you do it?"

"If I thought I could get out of working with Jeff without too much difficulty," Valerie replied. "I would do it. If I could accept an offer like that without two rival men involved, I would jump at the chance. I just don't know how I'm going to explain it to Jeff."

"Well, Dan hasn't offered you a position on his team — not yet." Charlene paced around the suite.

"There's still the chance Dan will go back to Phoenix when this case is over, and I'll go back to Denver and to Jeff, and everything else will go back to normal." She caught Charlene staring at her. "What? It could happen."

Charlene chuckled and shook her head.

"Okay. I won't argue with that. It could happen." She sat down on the couch next to Valerie and started digging into her travel bag.

"What do you think you're doing?" Valerie tried to wrestle the bag away from her.

Charlene pulled out a pair of lace trimmed underwear. She held them up and snorted with laughter.

"Where do you think you're going — the Playboy Mansion?"

Valerie jerked them out of her hand.

"Give me those. What do you think you're doing, going through my personal things?"

Charlene pulled out a thick file folder.

"I want to go over the case file. There must be something in here to give us a clue to this case."

She spread the file out on the coffee table, and Valerie couldn't stop herself from looking over her shoulder at the documents. Charlene turned the pages one after the other.

"Did you hear Dan say that compound of theirs was a major linkage between their mountain hideaway in Sonora and the shipping lanes in LA?"

"Sure, it was," Valerie replied. "They had to transport their human cargo somewhere. LA is a perfect solution to their problem."

Charlene shook her head.

"They weren't transporting to LA. They were passing these people on to the Chinese. They were selling them into slavery in Asia, and making a lot more money than if they just turned them loose in the good old US of A."

"He said that," Valerie replied, "but what does that have to do with our murder case?"

"Don't you see?" Charlene told her. "Who do you think he was meeting with at that motel? He could have been meeting with his contacts in the Chinese shipping end of things. He could have been arranging to deliver a batch of illegals for transport."

"So why did they kill him?" Valerie asked.

"Maybe they argued about money," Charlene replied. "Or maybe he insulted them. Or maybe he backed out of a deal they'd already made. It could have been anything."

"If it could have been anything," Valerie pointed out, "then you're really just making this up, aren't you? You have no reason to believe he was killed by Chinese shipping agents."

"I have no reason to believe he was killed by anybody," Charlene returned. "This theory is as good as any other."

Valerie shook her head.

"Donnelly knew the person Schneider planned to meet, even though he wouldn't tell us who it was. That means both he and Schneider knew that person well. I'll bet the killer was a member of their operation, someone Schneider trusted but who turned on him at the last moment."

Charlene bent her head over the file and chuckled.

"For someone who has too many things on her mind, you're thinking a lot about this case. Come on, and help me go through these papers. If we can find something to impress Mr. Mysterious, he'll love us even more than he already does."

Valerie made a face.

"Great. That's just what I need."

Charlene pushed a sheet of paper toward her.

"Here's the booking sheet for all the accomplices caught at the compound. All these men are in custody in the same building as Donnelly in San Antonio."

Valerie scanned the list.

"These are all European names. None of them would have a prayer of getting into The Machos, so we can strike that as our motive to murder Schneider."

Charlene held out another page.

"This lists everything confiscated from the compound—drugs, weapons, cash, even barrels of food. These guys had it all worked out."

"Of course they had food stores." Valerie picked up another sheet. "Take a look at this. They had over a thousand people imprisoned at this compound, including children down to the age of eighteen months. They would have had to feed them to keep them in condition for sale. They must have been going through the food like there's no tomorrow."

Charlene inspected the list.

"All the adults were women. That makes sense."

"But look at their ages," Valerie pointed out. "They're almost all in their thirties with young children. These women weren't going into the sex trade. They were breeding stock."

Charlene shuddered.

"I don't want to think about it."

Valerie turned away.

"I don't think the compound has anything to do with the murder."

Charlene's head shot up.

"Why not? Schneider was engaged in illegal activity. It makes sense that his death was connected to his business."

Valerie shook her head.

"I don't think so."

Charlene tossed her page down.

"If you want me to take your pronouncements seriously, you have to back them up with something. You're certain his death isn't connected to this compound, but you won't explain why."

"I can't explain why," she replied. "It's just a feeling I have. Call it a hunch."

Chapter 7

The three investigators stepped out of their hotel. Valerie fanned her face with her hand.

"It's stinkin' hot already, and it isn't even nine o'clock in the morning."

"Welcome to Arizona," Dan replied. "You've been on a Rocky Mountain high in Denver too long. If you think this is hot, you should try Phoenix some time."

Valerie panted.

"Let's get this over with."

They got into the unmarked car and drove through town to a dingy motel on the interstate, beyond the last neighborhood. Only half of the neon Lamplighter sign worked. It cast a depressing glow over the parking lot. Valerie scanned the building with a jaundiced eye.

"Charming."

Dan laughed.

"What did you expect a known criminal to pick for his safe haven?"

"He could afford the Hyatt," Charlene replied.

"We saw the manifest from the bust at the compound. Those guys had more than fifty thousand dollars sitting around their office in bundles of cash, and the bank statements the O-Line seized lists another three hundred thousand in accounts spread all over the western US."

"No amount of money in the world can buy you anonymity," Dan replied. "The same elements that would stop me from staying at the Hyatt would stop him staying there, too. Information flows both ways. The smugglers have agents all over the Southwest, but so do we. If he checked into the Regency and ordered room service and a hostess massage, we would have heard about it within a couple of hours. We would have him in a box at Fort Sam Houston with his friends, instead of at the Flagstaff city morgue."

Valerie turned to Charlene.

"That explains why the killer had to be someone Schneider trusted. He would be careful not to let anybody know his plans until he knew he was safe from capture."

"And yet he told Donnelly who he was meeting," Charlene pointed out.

"Then he must have trusted Donnelly, too," Valerie replied. "That's the only explanation."

Dan took a step toward the motel entrance.

"Well, we're not getting anywhere standing out here. Come on."

A blast of air conditioning nearly knocked them over backwards when they pushed open the reception office door.

A craggy old man switched off the volume on his TV behind the counter, but he left the set on. He hiked his pants up around his hips and leaned on the counter.

"What can I do for you?"

"We're here to investigate the death of Crockett Schneider," Dan told him.

This was the moment in most murder investigations when the officer flashed the subject his badge and ID, but Dan didn't bother. The man didn't notice the omission and regarded Dan with curiosity.

"He's the man found dead in his motel room," Dan explained.

The man nodded. "Yeah? What do you want to know about that?"

"Are you Arnold Harris?" Dan asked.

"That's right." He hiked up his pants again. "I'm the owner of this establishment."

"Then you're the one who told the police Emilio Donnelly visited Schneider in his room," Dan replied.

Harris looked back and forth between Dan and Valerie and Charlene. "What if I am?"

"How did you know to report Schneider's activities?" Dan asked. "How did you know Schneider was wanted? Our records show you didn't just call the local police, either. You called Patrick Sweeney, a Federal agent investigating illegal human traffic across the border. How did you know to contact him about Schneider?"

Harris shifted from one foot to the other.

"I've known Pat Sweeney for decades. I went to grade school with him."

"How did you know what he did for a living?" Dan asked.

"I didn't know he was some big shot agent working across the border," Harris replied. "I didn't know that until you told me just now. I saw him in a bar in town, and he bought me a beer. We caught up on old times. I knew he was a cop. That's all. I knew he wasn't no ordinary cop, though, since he never wore a uniform. He drove an old beat-up Ford Mustang with the door strung on with baling wire, and he wore ratty old cotton shirts, so I reckoned he was some kind of undercover spook. That's all."

Dan glanced over at Valerie.

"So you told him about Schneider."

"Sure," Harris replied.

"What made you do that?" Dan asked. "What made you think Schneider was the kind who ought to be reported to the cops?"

Harris broke into a choking laugh, but it sounded more like gagging. He must have been on five or six packs a day. His skin looked bad enough to be on ten packs a day.

He leered at Valerie and Charlene. "What gave it away? He was running from the law. Any moron could see that. He pulled in here at eleven o'clock at night in a rented car, but he had no picture ID. If his buddy hadn't paid in advance, I never would have let him have the room."

"Did his buddy front up and give you the money himself?" Dan asked.

"No way!" Harris shot back. "No one ever fronts up in this place unless they're dealing drugs or bringing in whores. No, this guy booked the room over the phone and he paid with a credit card."

Valerie frowned. "Credit card? Then you'll have a record of the card number and all the card holder's details — even what bank account it was drawn from."

Harris pulled a three-ring binder out from under the counter and slammed it down in front of them.

"There it is. Every receipt I've ever taken is in there. You want the details? Feel free to look it up."

"Thank you," Valerie replied. "I will."

"Tell us more about the guy who paid," Dan told him. "How do you know it wasn't the same guy who showed up on the day?"

"The guy on the phone told me the booking was for his friend," Harris replied.

"And he booked that particular night?" Valerie turned to Dan. "Then he knew exactly what date Schneider would be coming through. Something about this escape doesn't make sense. They had it all planned out, down to the day and hour."

"He knew the date, all right," Harris replied. "He told me his buddy would be coming through that day, but he didn't say he would wake me up out of a deep sleep and expect the royal treatment."

"What did he expect you to do besides let him into his room?" Dan asked.

"He wanted access to the internet," Harris replied.

"And he wanted a long distance account on the phone, and he wanted a wake-up call at five the next morning. I never get up at five in the morning, and I sure as shootin' wasn't gonna set my alarm to wake him up at that hour. He got rude about it until I threatened to call the cops to drag him off my property. That shut him up in a hurry."

The investigators exchanged glances. Dan let out a deep breath.

"So you told Sweeney about him."

"You bet I did," Harris replied.

"And you told Sweeney about Donnelly, too," Dan went on.

Harris scrunched up his furrowed brow.

"Who?"

"The guy who came to visit him," Dan replied. "You told Sweeney that Donnelly came to visit Schneider just before he died."

Harris waved his hand.

"Yeah, yeah. Sure, I told him."

"Someone else came to visit him after that," Dan told him.

Harris looked the other way and shrugged.

"Maybe they did and maybe they didn't. I don't keep track of everyone who comes to visit."

Dan snorted, but Valerie interrupted the conversation.

"You already reported who visited him to a Federal agent. Don't tell me you don't have some record of who else visited him."

Harris pulled out another three-ring binder and thumbed the pages.

"All right. There was another guy. He came in here and demanded a room right away, but he said it had to be that particular room."

He pointed down the long row of doors on the side of the building.

"He wouldn't take any room except the one right next to homeboy's room."

Valerie stared at him.

"Are you saying the second visitor booked into the room right next door to Schneider?"

"What else would I be saying?" Harris asked. "Why else would he want that room if he didn't want to visit that guy? Anyway, I saw them together. I saw him go into the room."

Valerie murmured to her friends.

"This must be the killer."

She faced Harris.

"Show us the booking records for the man who took the room next to Schneider's. Give us anything you've got on him."

Harris flipped open the first binder.

"It's all here. He paid with a credit card, too. His name and address, even his home phone number will be listed in this book."

He thumbed the pages and left greasy fingerprints on the corners. Then he stopped and ran his index finger down the page.

"Here's what you're looking for. Right. Now I remember. The man's name was Harold Henderson."

Chapter 8

Dan stormed out of the office and strode across the parking lot to his car. He almost yanked the door off its hinges getting it open. Valerie and Charlene hurried after him.

"Dan, wait!"

He didn't turn around.

"Wait a minute, Dan," Valerie cried. "Where are you going?"

Dan rounded on her. "I'm taking you two to the airport. I'm sending you back to Denver. I'll work this case out myself."

"You can't do that," Charlene told him. "You brought us in on this case, and we aren't leaving until we solve it. You must know that much about the Strikeforce Team. You can't bring us in and then send us home when things don't go your way."

Dan waved his hand toward the reception office. His eyes blazed.

"You heard what he said. My father is the prime suspect in Crockett Schneider's murder. I shouldn't be investigating this case at all. I have to go back to the head office in Phoenix and report to my superior officer. I'll have to withdraw myself from the case and let someone else take over."

He gritted his teeth and shook his fist at the motel.

"According to him, my father was the last person to meet Schneider before he was murdered."

"But we all know that's impossible," Valerie pointed out. "Your father was murdered at EdenCloud more than ten months ago. He couldn't have been here at the time Schneider was killed."

"What other explanation is there?" Dan asked.

Valerie pursed her lips.

"You're so emotional about this you're not thinking clearly. Your father couldn't have met him, which means someone else did, someone who used his name. Maybe someone knew you'd be investigating this case and they used your father's name to make sure you didn't find out who really killed Schneider."

He glared at her.

"Do you realize what you're saying?"

"Sure I do," Valerie replied. "Someone knew you'd have to withdraw yourself from this investigation as soon as your father's name came up. That's exactly why they used it. They wanted to drive you off the case so they could get away with murder."

"But who would do that?" he asked. "Who knew I would be investigating this case?"

"Donnelly knows you pretty well," Charlene chimed in.

"Have you had contact with him and his men before this? Maybe he found out about your father and used the name to undermine you."

"I've had him and his cronies in custody more times than I can count," Dan shrugged.

"They've wrangled the law every which way to get out of going to prison. Most of the time, they get deported back across the border, which for them is really like getting thrown back into the briar patch. It's the best possible place for them, and a few months later, they're back over here with a fresh transport. They know me as well as I know them."

"In that case," Valerie replied, "I think we can safely assume one of Donnelly's lieutenants used that name when they visited Schneider. They wanted to divert attention from the murder onto your father."

"I still have to withdraw," Dan told her. "Now that my father's name has entered the investigation, I have to step down. I can't get involved in this."

Valerie and Charlene exchanged glances. Then Valerie squared her shoulders and faced Dan.

"No, you don't. We're here, and we'll take over the investigation. You can stay on as an adviser while we take the lead."

He stared at her. Then he stared back and forth between her and Charlene. A faint smile spread over Charlene's face. Dan swallowed.

"Do you mean that?"

"If you back out now," Valerie replied, "this investigation is dead. If you leave for Phoenix, we'll go back to Denver, and the next investigator will have to start over from square one. Even if another O-Liner takes over for you, they won't know as much about this case as you do. Even in the short time we've been working with you, Charlene and I have learned more about this case than anyone could know starting from scratch. We should keep going if there's any possible way we can do it. Stick around and help us, and we'll crack this thing once and for all."

Dan arched his eyebrows at the two of them.

"She's right, Dan." Charlene nodded toward the motel. "Look, we're right here, at the scene of the crime, and we've got good information about Schneider's last hours. Let's not squander the gains we've made. Let's stick it out. Valerie and I will take the lead position. You can act as an expert deputy on the case."

Dan's head whipped around.

"Deputy?"

Charlene nodded.

"You'll be secondary, but Valerie and I will be the primary investigators."

Dan's shoulders slumped.

"I don't like it. This will be the first time in the history of the O-Line that one of us has acted as a deputy to any other law enforcement agent."

"Can you think of any other way to keep the investigation going?" Valerie asked.

Dan let out a shaky breath.

"No. In fact it's more than I could have hoped for under the circumstances."

Valerie smiled at him.

"Good. Then let's move on to the next step."

"Which is what?" he asked.

"Which is," she replied, "finding out who was the last person to meet Schneider. We know it wasn't your father."

"No one knows that better than we do," Charlene chimed in.

"Then who was it?" Dan asked. "This makes no sense at all."

"Either Donnelly played us around by telling us it was someone else when it was really him," Valerie replied, "or it *was* someone else who knew enough about you to use your father's name."

Dan shook his head.

"I can't think of anybody that could be."

Valerie waved her hand toward the car.

"Can we please get out of this heat while we talk about it? I can't think in this."

Dan stared at her. Then he smiled.

"Sure."

They slid into the car.

Dan started the motor and switched on the air conditioner, and the blast of icy air cooled all their tempers. Dan sighed.

"Thanks. I guess I lost it there for a minute."

Valerie managed to stop herself from touching his arm.

"Don't mention it. What are partners for? Besides, we can forgive you for reacting that way. I'm sure that whoever used your father's name planned to make you react exactly like that."

He sat in silence for a moment. Then he snorted.

"You're probably right."

"Let's talk about Donnelly," Valerie suggested.

"Could he have found out about your father during your previous contacts with him?"

Charlene spoke up from the back seat.

"He wouldn't have to find out anything other than his name. He could have found out Dan's father's name was Harold Henderson from a quick Google search," she pointed out.

"As a matter of fact, he wouldn't have to have any dealings with you in the past at all. All he would have to know is that you were investigating their trafficking operation. They could have kept your father's name in reserve for a situation just like this."

"Well, we can't fly back to San Antonio to ask him," Dan pointed out. "He would only deny it."

"Or he might spin some other stinkin' lie about how your father worked for them in the last months of his life," Valerie added. "He would say and do anything to throw us off the track. We should stay away from him and his men unless we have incontrovertible proof that one of them killed Schneider."

"There is one lead Harris gave us that we can look into." Charlene dropped the three-ring binder on the seat between Dan and Valerie.

"These are the credit card records for everyone who booked into the motel. We can track down this credit card that was used to pay for the room next door to Schneider's. We can find out who really did meet him right before he died."

Valerie spun around in her seat.

"Charlene! You're a genius."

"You're not the only person who knows how to solve a murder mystery, Valerie," Charlene replied. "I've been in this business this long enough to know what I'm doing."

Valerie flipped the pages in the binder.

"Here's the receipt for the room next to Schneider's." She paused. "Hmm. That's strange."

"What is?" Charlene asked.

"It doesn't list Harold Henderson as the cardholder," she replied.

Dan turned on her.

"What?"

She showed him the binder. "Look for yourself. The room was booked by Harold Henderson, but that's not the name on the credit card."

He peered down at the receipt.

"It says Visa Cardholder. That doesn't tell us anything."

Valerie smiled.

"Can you imagine your father having a card with that on it? Of course not. He was a successful businessman. He would have had his name on all his cards. If he checked into this motel — which we know he didn't — he would have used one of his own cards."

"He would have used his airpoints credit card," Dan replied. "He used it for everything so he could get the most airpoints."

"Exactly," Valerie replied. "So we need to track down who this card really belongs to."

"It says the issuing bank is Wells Fargo, Flagstaff branch." Dan threw the car into gear and sped out of the parking lot.

Valerie barely got her seat belt buckled before they hit the freeway. Dan dropped his foot on the accelerator and the Beamer purred toward Flagstaff. Valerie pulled out her computer and logged onto the Federal database. She typed in the credit card number.

"The card was issued to a Christopher Jenkins. He lives at 25 Saguaro Crescent."

"He won't be home right now," Charlene told her. "It's the middle of the day on a week day."

"The database lists his occupation as website designer," Valerie replied. "And it lists his business address as 25 Saguaro Crescent, too. He must work out of a home office."

Dan headed down an off ramp and wound through the neighborhoods.

"Here it is."

Valerie shut her laptop and examined the pristine houses and manicured lawns.

"This doesn't look like any place a trafficker would live."

"Expect the unexpected," Dan replied. "That's the one thing I've learned in this job. Nothing is as it seems."

He parked across the street from 25 Saguaro Crescent.

"What are you going to do?" Valerie asked. "Are you going to roll up to the door and start firing off questions?"

"Why not?" he asked. "It's the only way we're going to find out what happened."

At that moment, the door of the house opened. A woman dressed in a business suit came out, followed by three tidy children carrying backpacks and lunchboxes. Last of all, a man in sweat pants and a blue T-shirt came to the door.

He couldn't have been any taller than Valerie herself, and he wore glasses. He waved to the children with a cherubic smile, and they ran back into his arms. They kissed him and he kissed them. Then the woman laughed and kissed him, too.

The woman got into a minivan and buckled the children into their places.

They all waved to the man in the doorway, and he waved and blew them kisses. Valerie frowned.

"Am I the only one who thinks maybe we're on the wrong track?"

"He's no trafficker," Charlene muttered from the back seat. "I don't care what anybody says. He would never run the risk of losing his family to bump off Schneider."

"Then what was he doing in that motel room?" Dan asked.

"We have only Harris's word that he met with Schneider," Valerie pointed out.

"And he's got a home and family here in Flagstaff," Dan went on. "He wouldn't need to check into a motel room in his own home town."

"Maybe his card was stolen," Valerie suggested. "His name wasn't on the card, so anybody could have used it."

"There's one way to find out." Charlene swung her door open, and Dan and Valerie had to hurry to catch up with her.

The man spotted her striding across the street, and the smile evaporated off his face.

Charlene, on the other hand, gave him a big smile.

"Good morning." She flashed him her badge.

"What can I do for you, officer?" the man asked.

"Are you Christopher Jenkins?" she asked.

"Yes," he replied.

"We're investigating a string of credit card frauds," she told him. "We seem to have a misunderstanding, and we hoped you could clear it up."

He didn't relax.

"I'll help any way I can, but I was never involved in any fraud. I'm a law abiding citizen."

"I'm sure you are." Charlene waved her hand toward the end of the street where the minivan disappeared. "I saw you saying good-bye to your family. I can see you're a dedicated family man."

"You bet I am," he replied.

"Maybe you can shed some light on our problem, then," she replied. "It seems your credit card was used to book a motel room across town. Room 17 at the Lamplighter Motel. Do you know anything about that? If you didn't book it yourself, someone may have stolen your card or hacked the number. You could have a much bigger problem if someone stole your identity."

"No, that was me," he told her. "I booked the room and put it on my credit card. I'm a computer programmer. I would know if anybody stole my identity."

"You never know," Charlene replied. "These cases can develop faster than you think. Can you tell us why you booked the room when you have a home and family right here in Flagstaff?"

He didn't hesitate before answering.

"Sometimes I get a big contract and I have a tight deadline," he told her. "I need to work a lot, sometimes around the clock, without the distractions of kids screaming and banging on my office door wanting books read to them and everything else that strikes their fancy. When that happens, I get myself a quiet motel room where I can work in peace."

Charlene glanced at Valerie.

"So you didn't see anybody else while you were booked at the Lamplighter?"

Jenkins shook his head.

"I don't see anybody when I do these stints. That's the whole point of leaving home, so I don't see anybody. If I didn't want to see my own children during that time, I wouldn't make time to see anybody else. I can tell you that."

"Do you know anybody named Crockett Schneider?" Charlene asked. "Does that name ring any bells to you?"

Jenkins frowned.

"I can't say that it does. I don't know anybody by that name."

Charlene narrowed her eyes.

"Are you absolutely certain you didn't talk to anybody or leave the room while you were there? Did you speak to anybody at all after you checked in"

Jenkins rubbed his chin.

"I might have exchanged a few words with the guy in the room next door. I ordered a pizza, and when I came to the door to pay the delivery guy, the door to the next room opened. This dude with filthy hair asked me if I had any extra batteries for the TV remote. I said he could have mine, since I wasn't watching TV."

"Did you go into his room?" Charlene asked.

Jenkins burst into a grin.

"Actually, I did, now that you mention it. He couldn't figure out how to change the batteries. Can you believe that? I had to go into his room to do it for him. He must have been living under a rock for the last thirty years."

Charlene grinned.

"He was, sort of." She nodded and turned away. "Thank you very much for your help, Mr. Jenkins. I'm glad your credit card is safe."

Chapter 9

Dan slammed his door extra hard when they parked outside the Lamplighter Motel again.

"Just wait until I get my hands on that old bugger."

"Wait a minute, Dan." Valerie pointed to the end of the building. "Take a look at that."

"What about it?" Dan asked.

"Look at the numbers on the doors," Valerie told him.

"They only go up to number 17. The rest of the rooms must be around the other side of the building."

"So what?" Dan snapped.

"I think I understand," Charlene replied.

"Jenkins told us he came here for quiet, and Harris said he requested that room specifically. We assumed he requested it to be near Schneider, who was in room 16, but if Jenkins told us the truth, he picked that room because it's at the far end of the building, away from the street. It would be the quietest room in the whole motel."

"Exactly," Valerie exclaimed.

"We know that they talked to each other, and Jenkins went into Schneider's room to change the batteries for his TV remote. Harris must have seen them together, and when we asked who Schneider met before he died, he remembered Jenkins. Mystery solved."

"Not quite," Dan replied. "How do you explain my father's name on the booking receipt?"

"Harris told us he used your father's name," Charlene reminded him. "And Harris wrote the name into the binder. Maybe Harris had some connection to your father."

Valerie whirled around. She pointed at Dan and clapped her hands.

"That's it!"

Dan and Charlene exchanged glances.

"What's it?"

Valerie tore the car door open and grabbed her computer and the receipt binder. She hurried toward the reception office.

"Come on. We've got him right where we want him."

Charlene stumbled after her.

"What are you talking about?"

Valerie didn't stop until she burst into the office and surprised Arnold Harris behind the counter. The TV blasted at full volume, and he couldn't decide whether to hitch up his pants or turn down the TV. In the end, he ran his fingers through his hair, tugged his pants into position, and flicked off the TV. He put out his hand for the binder.

"So you brought it back. Good."

Valerie pulled it away from him.

"I think we might hold onto it for a while."

"You can't hold onto it," he told her. "I need it to run my business. You can't confiscate it without a warrant."

"You won't need it to run your business," she replied. "Besides, we can confiscate it without a warrant if we believe a crime has been committed, and this is evidence."

He frowned.

"I don't know about that. Anyway, I didn't commit any crime, so you can't take it."

"We have reason to believe you did commit a crime," she replied. "Even if you didn't have anything to do with Crockett Schneider's death — and I think I can prove that you did — you doctored your records to implicate a dead man in his murder. That's fraud and conspiracy, not to mention obstruction of justice."

He shifted from one foot to the other.

"I don't know what you're talking about."

Valerie set her computer on the counter and opened it. She turned it so he could see the screen.

"What's this?" He sounded puzzled.

"This is the Federal database," she replied. "This is where members of Federal agencies can look up information on victims and suspects and investigate crimes."

Harris peered at the screen.

"This page says Crockett Schneider."

Valerie waved her hand.

"I know. It only opened to that page because it's the last thing I looked at before I came in here. The page I wanted to show you is a different one."

Charlene murmured into Valerie's ear.

"What are you trying to do?"

Valerie ignored her. She typed something into the search window and hit Enter.

"This is a page on Harold Henderson. He's the man whose name you put down in the booking record for the room next to Schneider's. I'm sure you remember telling us about that."

Harris's eyes skimmed back and forth between the investigators' faces, but he didn't answer.

"You see, this man here," she gestured toward Dan, "is Captain Dan Henderson. He's Harold Henderson's son."

She paused for her words to take effect.

"Harold Henderson was a successful businessman, but most people don't know he was also an undercover operative for an elite Federal agency called the Strikeforce Investigation Team."

Harris recovered his composure.

"I never heard of it."

Valerie shrugged.

"That doesn't matter, because I'm going to explain everything you need to know. Colonel Tomlinson of the Strikeforce Team recruited Henderson, Senior, to work undercover to bust a criminal organization in the northern New Mexico mountains. Colonel Tomlinson had to brief Henderson on the situation in a secret location unknown to anybody else. But since Henderson lived in Phoenix and Tomlinson worked out of Denver, they had to meet somewhere in the middle. They chose Flagstaff."

Charlene gasped.

"Valerie!"

Valerie smiled at her partner.

"After we came back from EdenCloud, I did some reading up on Harold Henderson. I just remembered he met Colonel Tomlinson in Flagstaff before he went up to the retreat center."

She pointed to her computer screen.

"See? It says right there under investigation-related expenses. The Team bank account was tapped to pay for one room for Colonel Tomlinson and one room for Harold Henderson at the Lamplighter Motel."

Charlene and Dan bent over the screen.

"Well, what do you know!"

Harris looked the other way.

"This doesn't prove anything."

Valerie stood back from her computer.

"Why did you change the names on your booking record? Why did you change Christopher Jenkins's name to Harold Henderson?"

Harris hiked up his pants again.

"You can't pin this on me. You've got nothing. I've got a couple thousand names in my booking record. You can't nail me for any crime."

Valerie pursed her lips.

"Please, Mr. Harris. Make it easy on yourself. Tell us the truth. If you had any extenuating circumstances that could lead you to kill Crockett Schneider, you could get your sentence reduced. Just tell us what happened and we'll see what we can do to help you."

Arnold Harris set his poochy lips in a pout, and his eyes flashed from Valerie to Dan to Charlene and back to Valerie.

"I'll tell you what. I know something even better that will reduce my sentence."

With lightning speed, he bent over and pulled something out from under the counter. Valerie only had time to recognize the sawn-off twenty gauge shotgun before she dove for cover. The old man could move fast, though, and he whipped the gun around and fired before Dan or Charlene could act. The gun went off in Dan's face, and he staggered backwards.

A disgusting gurgle rumbled out of Dan's chest. He stumbled away from the blast and crashed into the office window. His weight shattered the glass, and he toppled backwards onto the sidewalk, where he landed on his back on a carpet of broken glass.

Blue smoke filled the office, and by the time Valerie dared to look up, Arnold Harris and his shotgun were gone.

She crawled through the glass to Dan. He lay with his eyes closed, and his chest didn't rise and fall with breath. Valerie laid her hand on his arm.

"Dan? Can you hear me?" He didn't answer. A lump stuck in her throat. This couldn't be the end. She couldn't lose him like this.

A screech of tires brought her head around, and a black Mazda hatchback peeled out of the parking lot with Arnold Harris at the wheel. Valerie fumbled for her phone, but a death rattle brought her attention back to Dan. She bent over him expecting to see a gush of blood spill out of his mouth and nose and chest. Instead, he gagged and coughed and spluttered. Then he opened his eyes.

"That bastard!" he growled. "I'll tear his arms off for this."

Valerie stared down at him.

"Dan?"

Dan peeked at her through squinted eyelids.

"Gotta... gotta get up. Gotta... get after him. Can't let him get away."

He tried to sit up but only collapsed back on the pavement in a paroxysm of coughing. Valerie laughed out loud in pure relief. He was alive.

"You're hurt, Dan. We have to call an ambulance. We should contact your superior officer, too."

Dan pounded his chest with his fist.

"I'm all right. Just give me a minute to catch my breath. Then we gotta get after him. We have to catch him."

"But how...?" Valerie stammered.

Dan stole a sidelong glance at her. Then he pulled the tattered edges of his shirt apart. Instead of a morass of bullet holes and gore, an even mat of bright blue fibers covered his chest. Five gleaming circles of silver metal dotted the surface.

"Kevlar." Dan grinned at her. "After what happened at the lock-up at Fort Sam, I thought I better come prepared."

Valerie stared down into his face. Then she couldn't stop herself from kissing him.

"You're a true Boy Scout."

Dan struggled to his feet.

"No time for that now. Come on. We gotta catch him."

Valerie helped him up, and they ran back to their car. Charlene slid into the back seat.

"He's got the jump on us. How are we going to find out where he went?"

Dan hit the gas and tossed his phone to Valerie in the passenger seat.

"Dial star 89."

The engine and tire noise blotted out every sound.

"What?" she screamed.

He bent his head closer to her ear and thundered, "Star 89."

Valerie punched the number into the phone, and an operator answered. "XQT06."

Valerie stammered her reply.

"I'm Valerie Inglewood from the Strikeforce Team. I'm working with Captain Dan Henderson in Flagstaff."

The operator didn't miss a beat.

"What can I do for you, Agent Inglewood?"

Valerie's spirits soared.

"We're in pursuit of a suspect. He just fled the Lamplighter Motel, and we're following on westbound Interstate 40."

"I'm scrambling a chopper now, Agent Inglewood," the operator chirped. "Continue on Interstate 40 heading west. I have Captain Henderson's phone number, and I'll advise you of any change in direction. Thank you." The line went dead.

Valerie stared at the phone.

"She's scrambling a chopper. She said to keep on going west on 40."

"Good," Dan replied.

"How did she know where Harris was?" Valerie asked.

Dan didn't have a chance to answer. An enormous Black Hawk helicopter rose out of the horizon and swooped down on them. It buzzed over the highway, made a pass over their car and banked away again.

Valerie squinted into the distance.

"Where's Harris?"

Charlene jumped forward in her seat and pointed through the windshield.

"There he is!"

Valerie followed the direction of her hand and gasped out loud.

"He's in the oncoming lane! The operator said she would advise us if he changed direction."

"She would only advise us if she wanted *us* to change direction," Dan told her. "She must have wanted us to keep going this way."

At that moment, the chopper appeared above their heads. The wash from its propeller blades shook the car. Dan yanked the steering wheel to keep it tracking straight. Then the chopper banked again and descended onto the highway right in front of Arnold Harris's car.

Harris's eyes popped out of his head at the sight of the giant black helicopter setting down in front of him. The chopper blocked the highway, and he jerked his steering wheel to avoid crashing into it. He crossed two lanes of traffic and hit the grassy verge between the east and west bound highways. He bounced over the verge and charged straight for Dan's car.

Dan hit the brakes and drove his steering wheel hard to the left. The BMW skidded sideways, but Dan never lost control. He sent the car into a perfect slide into the verge, and Harris's Mazda smashed head on into the side door. The door crumpled and smashed Valerie across her seat into Dan's shoulder. In an instant, both cars stood still, with a cloud of steam billowing from under Harris's hood.

Behind the shattered windshield, Harris waved steam out of his face and peered at his collapsed front end. Dan chuckled.

"I love it when a plan comes together." He slid out of his seat and extended his hand to Valerie. "Come on. You won't be getting out that way."

She scooted behind the wheel and took his hand. He helped her out of the car, and they walked around to Harris's door. Dan opened it.

"Arnold Harris, you're under arrest for the murder of Crockett Schneider."

Harris pretended to struggle when Dan pulled him out of the car, but he didn't really try to resist. There was no point.

"You don't understand. He was dangerous."

"Tell us what happened," Valerie told him. "If you can show he threatened you or made you fear for your life in some way, you might not do any time for killing him."

"He didn't threaten me," Harris replied. "He didn't have to. You could tell that guy was dangerous just by looking at him. I never saw a more dangerous guy in my life, except maybe that guy you mentioned before."

Valerie frowned. "Who? You don't mean Harold Henderson."

"That's exactly who I mean," he replied.

Dan ground his teeth, but Valerie spoke up before he could respond.

"Henderson wasn't dangerous."

"Oh, yes, he was!" Harris shot back. "I've seen the most dangerous characters in the world in this job, and he was the shiftiest, crookedest character I've ever seen. Why do you think I picked him to finger for this?"

Valerie and her friends exchanged glances.

"You still haven't told us why you killed Schneider."

Harris glared at her. Then he let his chin fall onto his chest.

"All right. I'll tell you. I guess there's nothing else to do about it. He came storming into my office full of piss and vinegar."

"Who did?" Charlene asked.

"Schneider," Harris replied. "I couldn't even understand what on earth he was raving about between spit flying out of his mouth and his arms waving a mile a minute. Finally, I figured out he couldn't get the stupid TV in his room to work."

Valerie frowned.

"This sounds familiar."

"I said maybe the batteries were getting low," Harris went on. "Well, you'd think I just suggested I sleep with his wife or something. He went ballistic. I thought he was going to attack me then and there. He threw the TV remote down on the counter and said they were fresh batteries, and he changed them for the batteries in the remote from the room next door."

Charlene nodded.

"So that's how you knew he met with the guy next door."

"Sure," Harris replied. "He told me so himself. He said the guy came into his room to change them. So I said maybe the remote itself has a short. He ranted and raved about something or other, so I took the remote from my own TV, that I knew for certain worked just fine, with fresh batteries and everything, and I took it to his room. I used it on his TV, and it worked."

"What did he say to that?" Valerie asked.

"He got even more mad," Harris told her.

"He smashed his fist through the wall and knocked a lamp over. He asked if I thought he was stupid or something, and he threatened to sue me if he caught me charging him for fixing the remote."

"Did he attack you at all?" Valerie asked.

Harris shifted from one foot to the other.

"No, nothing like that."

"So what made you decide to kill him?" Charlene asked.

"I said I'd had enough of his attitude, and I started to leave," Harris replied.

"He wasn't finished with me, though, and he jumped in front of me. I dodged to get around him so I could get out the door, and he tried to head me off. He tripped over the cord from the lamp he'd just knocked over. He fell over and bumped his head on the corner of the table. He came up foaming at the mouth and shouting threats and I... I guess I lost it, too."

"What do you mean, you lost it?" Valerie asked.

"I... don't remember exactly what happened," Harris stammered. "I only knew that I couldn't stay in that room any longer. I had to get away from him. He was getting more and more dangerous, and every time I tried to get out, he cut me off. I got scared, so I..." He stopped.

"You killed him," Charlene added. "You stabbed him with a knife."

Harris stared down at the ground.

"I had a pocket knife in my pocket. I pulled it out and... I guess I..."

Valerie turned to Dan.

"We shouldn't question him any more until he's got his lawyer present."

Dan clenched his jaw.

"One more question. Why did you change the booking record from Christopher Jenkins to Harold Henderson?"

"I told you," Harris replied. "Henderson was dangerous. I don't care what you say about him. He was a vicious criminal. I could tell that by looking at him. I had to blame Schneider's death on someone, and no one would believe that pansy Jenkins killed him, not even if they knew he went into Schneider's room. After I... I went back to the office, and I got the idea of blaming Jenkins for the... for the..."

Valerie nodded and patted his arm.

"We understand. Take your time."

Harris swallowed hard.

"I got the idea of blaming Jenkins, but I needed to change him into someone the police would believe really killed Schneider. I flipped the pages of my receipt book, and I caught sight of Harold Henderson's name. I made a snap decision to switch the names. That's all. It was stupid, I know, but…"

Valerie turned away.

"We've heard enough. Don't say any more until you talk to your lawyer."

Dan took hold of Harris's arm.

"Come with me. We'll take you into town."

He handcuffed Harris and strapped him into the helicopter. Then he met Valerie and Charlene back at the BMW.

"I'll take him into town and get him booked."

"We still don't know who Schneider was going to meet after Donnelly left," Valerie told him.

"We'll probably never know," Dan replied. "He said it was someone in the trade, so it could have been someone from their own operation. We could already have the person in custody at Fort Sam Houston."

"I don't suppose Harris will end up there," Valerie remarked.

Dan shook his head. "He'll probably get off on a self-defense plea. Schneider repeatedly stopped him when he tried to leave the room, and he destroyed Harris's property to terrorize him. Harris told us he thought Schneider was dangerous, and he was probably right."

"Why do you think he considered your father dangerous?" Valerie asked.

Dan shrugged.

"Maybe he saw what he wanted to see. Maybe my father acted shifty and tense when he met Colonel Tomlinson. I wouldn't blame him if he did. Either way, he's going to the local jail. He doesn't need Federal custody."

"I guess that's the end of the case, then," Valerie told him. "What will you do after you drop him off downtown?"

"Take the Beamer back to the hotel." He tossed Valerie the keys. "I'll meet you there later. Do me a favor and don't pop a tire on the way."

"This car belongs to the O-Line," she pointed out. "We shouldn't be driving it."

"Don't worry about that," he replied.

"I'm officially deputizing you. Take the car and meet me back at the hotel."

She smiled up at him.

"Aren't you supposed to be our deputy?"

He snorted.

"That'll be the day."

Chapter 10

Valerie leaned back in her seat and sipped her champagne. She'd never tasted anything like it. Dan came strolling down the aisle and laughed out loud when he caught sight of her.

"Making yourself comfortable, I see."

Valerie sat up straight.

"I'm just enjoying my last few minutes in the lap of luxury. I can't imagine what it must be like to work in this kind of environment. It doesn't even feel like law enforcement."

"Why don't you give it a try?" Dan asked. "Why don't you come work for the O-Line?"

Valerie cocked her head.

"Don't tell me you do the recruiting for your team, too."

"No, but I could convince my superior officer," he replied. "I've already shown my team your credentials. You were right about this case in the face of everything Charlene and I said about it. You saw right through it, and you figured out the murder had nothing to do with Schneider's business. When my people hear how you cracked this case, they'll want you to come on board with us."

Valerie looked away.

"I think I better debrief with Colonel Tomlinson before I do anything else."

Dan shrugged.

"Of course. All three of us have to debrief with Colonel Tomlinson."

"You might want to mention to him in your debrief that you're trying to poach me," Valerie told him. "Not that it would make much difference in the end. I suppose your superior officer outranks Colonel Tomlinson. What is he — a general or something?"

Dan fixed her with his piercing gaze.

"She's a woman, and yes, she does outrank him. She's Secretary of State."

Valerie's mouth fell open.

"Secretary of..." She shut her mouth and took another sip of her drink. "Never mind. I shouldn't be surprised by anything you say or do."

He settled into the seat and elbowed her in friendly companionship.

"If you wanted to come over to the O-Line, no one could stop you. You've proven yourself more than capable. No one will order you to come and no one will stop you from coming if you want to do it. The decision will be yours and no one else's."

"Why would I want to leave the Strikeforce Team?" she asked. "I worked for almost eight years to get this position. I wouldn't throw it away."

"People work a lot longer than that to join the O-Line," he told her. "The cases are bigger and tougher, and the stakes are higher. You're fighting for our country's future. Our national security is riding on us."

Valerie shrugged.

"I'll think about it."

He leaned toward her.

"And we would be together. Don't forget that."

Valerie blushed.

"I can't forget Jeff Everson, either. I'm already with him on the Strikeforce Team. I don't need to change teams to get a man."

He laughed again.

"You don't have to do anything to get a man, Valerie. You can get any man you shake your little finger at. I'm only saying, if you joined the O-Line, we would be together. You wouldn't have to choose between me and Jeff Everson. He would be a thing of the past."

Valerie started to say something, but he leaned the rest of the way over and kissed her. Before she could stop herself, her lips melted against his, and a tidal wave of excitement and desire swept the supports out from under her.

Why should she go back to Denver, to Jeff? Why shouldn't she throw caution to the wind and go to Phoenix with Dan to join the O-Line? What possible reason did she have to hold herself back?

He sensed the change in her and pressed against her. His arm burrowed behind her back and pulled her off the seat toward him. He took the champagne glass out of her hand and scooped her into his lap.

Her body rose to meet him and heaved against his chest. She belonged with him. Her body belonged in rapt embrace with him, with nothing separating them from each other and nothing blocking her from merging with him.

She wrapped her arms around his neck and gave herself over to the passion of his kiss. Let him take her. Let him sweep her off her feet and wash everything else away into the past. Let Jeff and the Strikeforce Team and Charlene and Denver disappear and leave only him in their place. She could live with that.

All of a sudden, Charlene popped her head up over the seat back in front of them. She waved her phone at them. "I hate to interrupt this steamy love scene, but I just got a text from Colonel Tomlinson. We're going back to Denver to brief him on the conclusion of the case, and then we're meeting up with Jeff and Tiko. We're teaming up with them for our next assignment."

Dan stared at Valerie.

"There you go. You'll be back with your boyfriend, and you can forget all about me."

"Wrong again, Big Boy," Charlene crowed. "There's a gang of bikers running loose on the streets of El Paso. They've killed four sheriff's deputies so far and twenty civilians. They've set up a stronghold in an abandoned warehouse, and no one can get near 'em. Valerie and I and Jeff and Tiko are being assigned to tackle 'em, and you've been reassigned as tactical support. We're all going to be working together on this, and you're coming with us."

The End.

Don't miss Valerie's next case, in "From Bad to Worse" – you'll find a taste of that book just after the 'About the Author' section!

About the Author

T.K. Wilde is a long term writer, who writes both fiction and non-fiction, under a number of pen names.

A particular fondness for mysteries, action, and non-standard female characters resulted in this series – we hope you enjoy it!

Books in the Valerie Inglewood Series

The series, in reading order, is

1. Bad Moon Rising

2. One Bad Apple

3. Bad Blood

4. Bad Intent
(this book)

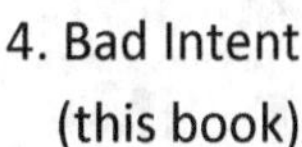

5. From Bad to Worse

Here is your preview of Book 5 in the series

STRIKEFORCE AGENT
VALERIE INGLEWOOD

FROM BAD TO WORSE

T.K. WILDE

Chapter 1

Machine gun fire peppered Charlene Brockworth's windshield. Valerie Inglewood dove for cover and spat out dust onto the floor in front of the passenger seat.

"What the....?"

Bullets popped against the car's metal body. Charlene stretched across the seat and jammed a clip into her semi-automatic pistol. She bellowed over the din.

"Where's your boyfriend?"

"How should I know?" Valerie shouted back. Then she cocked her head. "Which one do you mean?"

Charlene broke into a big grin and snapped back the slide on her pistol.

"I don't care. Anyone will do as long as they give us some back up here."

Valerie put her hand behind her back for her own weapon, but as she did so, her head broke the line of the dashboard, and a fresh spray of bullets pelted the car. She ducked for cover.

"I don't know where they are and I'm not looking for them in this heat."

"What did you expect?" Charlene shouted back. "Colonel Tomlinson told us we were walking into a gang war. This is it."

"What did I expect?" Valerie shot back. "I expected to unpack my suitcase and have a cup of iced tea down at the local taqueria. That's what I expected. I didn't expect we'd be pinned down by gunfire the minute we rolled into town."

Charlene gripped her weapon with both hands.

"Well, we can't spend the next week cowering here in fright. We have to get out of here and find Jeff and Tiko."

"What about Dan Henderson?" Valerie asked.

Charlene shook her head.

"They've all got their own cars, so one of two things has happened. Either they're pinned down by gunfire just like we are, or they're not. Either way, we have to get out of here. We need their help or they need ours. We can't stay here."

"Well, I don't see you getting off the couch," Valerie pointed out. "If you're so hot to race out there and take a bullet for the cause, I can't wait to see you try it."

Charlene glanced out the windshield, but she didn't raise her head.

"No."

"No what?" Valerie asked.

"No, I don't really want to race out there and take a bullet," Charlene replied.

Valerie rolled her eyes.

"Well, hallelujah! We're making progress."

Charlene narrowed her eyes at her partner.

"Let's hear your suggestions on how we're going to get out of here."

"I don't have any." Valerie scanned the car. "Here we are — or I should say, here I am — discovering dust bunnies on the floor of a car in El Paso while some unseen assailant shoots the car to pieces. I'm not sticking my neck out at a time like this. No way! I'll stay right here, thank you very much."

"Well, how do you propose we get out of here?" Charlene demanded. "We can't just lie here and wait for the desperadoes to come and cap us."

"What makes you think they'll cap us?" Valerie asked.

"Well, they sure as blazes won't just stop shooting and go home for siesta, will they?" Charlene shot back. "Once they realize we're cowed into submission, they'll sneak up on this car to finish the job."

Valerie looked around and nodded. "You've got a point there."

Charlene settled back on the seat.

"Thank you."

"All the shooting is coming from over there," Valerie pointed out. "We might be able to sneak out the other door."

Charlene followed the direction of Valerie's nod. "Okay. I'm starting to see the light at the end of the tunnel."

"See if you can kick the door open," Valerie told her. "If the desperadoes are all on that side of the car, the coast should be clear."

"And if it isn't," Charlene pointed out, "then I'm Swiss Cheese."

Valerie grinned.

"You're in luck."

Charlene arched her eyebrows.

"Why's that?"

Valerie dropped her voice to a murmur. "I'm bread sticks." Then she burst out laughing.

Charlene narrowed her eyes.

"I'm gonna kill you for this."

Valerie jerked her chin toward the door.

"Kick the door open. Stop stalling."

Charlene shook her head and took a fresh grip on her weapon.

"First thing I'm doing when we get back to Denver is requesting a change of partner."

Valerie gasped.

"Come on, Charlene. Give me a break for trying to lighten up the situation."

Charlene shook her head.

"I'm not talking to you anymore."

She turned away and scooted down the seat so that her bent legs rested against the driver's door. She took a deep breath.

"Here goes."

Charlene kicked the door handle to release the latch. She bunched her legs up to her chest. Then with all her might she kicked out at the door.

It flew open and immediately swung shut. It slammed so hard it latched itself again. But, in the few seconds it had hung open, Valerie and Charlene had peeked out across a five-foot gap to an Olive Garden restaurant, standing deserted across the sidewalk.

The gap between their car and the restaurant beckoned to them with open arms. Valerie's spirits soared.

"This is it! This is the way out we've been looking for!"

Charlene turned on her.

"We are not going out there. No way on God's green earth are we going out there in a hail of gunfire. Those desperadoes, as you call 'em, could be lying in wait for us to try something just like this. They could be waiting to turn us into chocolate fondue the minute we stick our noses outside this car."

"Don't you mean Swiss cheese?" Valerie asked.

Charlene pulled her head down between her shoulders.

"I'm not going out there, and I forbid you to go out there, either, Valerie. It's suicide."

Valerie stopped smiling.

"Listen, Charlene. You said yourself staying in this car is suicide, and if Jeff and Dan and Tiko are out there somewhere, they could need us just as much as we need them. We have to get out of this car some way or another, and I don't see any other way to do it. Do you?"

Charlene pursed her lips, but didn't answer.

"Would you like me to go first?" Valerie asked.

Charlene's head shot up. Valerie caught a glimmer of relief in her eyes. Then she looked down at the floor.

"No, no. I'm the senior officer. You're supposed to be training under me for another six months."

Valerie snorted.

"Yeah, right."

Charlene stared at the door.

"I'll go."

Valerie shifted her weapon in her hand and grabbed hold of Charlene's sleeve.

"Come on. Get off the seat and let me go first."

Charlene waved her hand.

"No, no…"

Valerie almost hauled her off the seat.

"Get down before I thump you into submission."

Charlene tried to yank her sleeve out of Valerie's grip, but to no avail.

"Hey! Let go of me. This is gross insubordination."

Valerie didn't let go.

"If you hesitate at all, you could get us both killed. Now get down and let me go first. This was my daffy idea. If the desperadoes are laying for us out there, I'll be the first to catch it. You'll be alive and well in this car to try Plan B."

Charlene rolled her eyes and hooted.

"That's just flamin' great!"

Valerie took hold of both her arms and forced her off the seat onto the passenger side floor. Then she took Charlene's place on the seat. She rolled over onto her back and took a two-handed grip on her weapon. She flexed her legs and set them against the door. She shot Charlene a wicked grin.

"Now sit back and watch the master at work."

She flicked the door handle with her toe, and the latch gave way. The door hung free. Valerie took a deep breath, pulled back her legs, and kicked as hard as she could. The door flew open the way it had before, but this time, it didn't swing shut.

Valerie scooted off the seat and dropped to the ground behind the door with her weapon pointed outward into space.

No-one shot at her. No-one could even see her crouching behind the door. She swept the open patch of street in front of her with her pistol, but even the machine gun fire on the other side of the car dropped off to the occasional burp. Beyond the car door, the restaurant door stood open. Only a few feet of exposed space separated Valerie from relative safety.

She coiled her legs under her and launched herself across the gap.

Whoever was shooting up their car spotted her and rained another torrent of bullets at her, but by then it was too late. She dove into the Olive Garden, skated across the floor, and came to rest in front of the salad bar.

When she got onto her hands and knees, she spotted Charlene crouched behind the car door. Valerie hadn't done her any favors by going first. The desperadoes would be watching for the next person to try the same trick. Charlene hesitated a lot longer than Valerie had to work up the nerve to make the run for safety.

She blew through her mouth several times until Valerie waved her over with her pistol. What was taking so long? All at once, Charlene shot out of her hiding place. The explosion of gunfire started the instant she appeared from behind the door, and the noise confused her. She raised her arms around her head and, for a fraction of a second, took her eyes off her destination. That second was all it took to make her stumble and fall in the middle of the gap, right where she would be exposed to the worst of the gunfire.

Valerie shot forward to help her, but hundreds of bullets whizzed across the gap. She couldn't leave the restaurant the way she'd come, but she couldn't help Charlene without breaking her own cover. Charlene lay flat on her face on the sidewalk with only her own arms to protect her from the bullets. Valerie hid behind the door jamb. She dared not even peek out to see when or where she might get a break in the fight to help her partner.

Then, with no warning, the machine gun gave one final burp of fire and a click rang through the street.

Voices shouted through the silence, along with several loud metallic clangs. The desperadoes were reloading their magazine. Valerie would never find a better time to act.

She set her own weapon down on the ground as fast as she could without dropping it. She would need both hands to be any good to her much larger partner. Then she darted out onto the sidewalk. Without a word, she laid hold of Charlene's jacket and dragged her across the concrete toward the Olive Garden.

"Hey! Let me go!" Charlene cried. "What do you think you're doing?"

Valerie didn't stop.

"I'm saving your life."

The voices shouted louder and faster than ever. They'd seen her, and they'd be working double time to get their gun up and running again. Before she got halfway across the sidewalk, the first explosion rocked the foundations under them. Valerie crouched as best she could, but she couldn't crouch very well and pull Charlene at the same time. She opted to risk the machine gun fire to get her partner and herself to safety once and for all.

Charlene was a lot heavier than she looked, though. Valerie puffed and strained, and every muscle fiber screamed from the effort. Charlene kicking and struggling didn't help much, either. Bursts of gunfire rattled against the car and shattered the restaurant windows, but Valerie couldn't stop now. With one last heave, she towed Charlene across the threshold to the safety of the salad bar.

Charlene rolled over with her teeth bared.

"Don't you dare pull a stunt like that ever again."

Valerie laid her hand on Charlene's shoulder and gazed into her eyes.

"You're welcome."

Find out what happens next-

Make sure to get your copy as soon as its released !

IN THE MIDDLE OF A GANG WAR, BEING
A HOSTAGE IS BAD FOR YOUR HEALTH.
FROM BAD TO WORSE
STRIKEFORCE AGENT
VALERIE INGLEWOOD
T.K. WILDE

Other Books from Dreamstone Publishing

Dreamstone publishes books in a wide variety of categories – here are some of our other bestselling non fiction books:-

Moving Beyond the Unspoken Grief:
A doctor's memoir of her own IVF
journey as a patient
By Dr Sarah Lnyy

Should I Quit?
Resilience for a turbulent world
By Mike Gordon

"Icebreakers : How to Empower,
Motivate and Inspire Your Team,
Through Step-by-Step Activities That
Boost Confidence, Resilience and
Create Happier Individuals"
By Di McMath

All Books available from all Amazon sites and other book stores, and available for Kindle too!

And here are some of our bestselling romance books from Arietta Richmond.

Be first to know when our next books are coming out – sign up for our newsletter at

http://www.dreamstonepublishing.com